Cross

www.**books**at**transworld**.co.uk

KEN BRUEN

Cross

BANTAM PRESS

LONDON · TORONTO · SYDNEY · AUCKLAND · JOHANNESBURG

TRANSWORLD PUBLISHERS
61–63 Uxbridge Road, London W5 5SA
a division of The Random House Group Ltd

First published in Great Britain
in 2007 by Bantam Press
a division of Transworld Publishers

Copyright © Ken Bruen 2007

Ken Bruen has asserted his right under the Copyright, Designs and
Patents Act 1988 to be identified as the author of this work.

This book is a work of fiction and, except in the case of historical fact, any resemblance to
actual persons, living or dead, is purely coincidental.

A CIP catalogue record for this book
is available from the British Library

ISBNs 9780593057278 (cased)
978059305055137 (tpb)

Addresses for Random House Group Ltd companies outside the UK can
be found at: www.randomhouse.co.uk
The Random House Group Ltd Reg. No. 954009

The Random House Group Ltd makes every effort to ensure that the
papers used in its books are made from trees that have been legally sourced
from well-managed and credibly certified forests. Our paper procurement
policy can be found at: www.randomhouse.co.uk/paper.htm

Typeset in 12/16pt Sabon by
Kestrel Data, Exeter, Devon

Printed and bound in Great Britain by
Clays Ltd, Bungay, Suffolk

2 4 6 8 10 9 7 5 3 1

www.booksattransworld.co.uk

For
David Zeltersman . . . True Noir,
Jim Winter . . . a Writer of Dark Beauty,
Gerry Hanberry . . . the Poet of the Western World.

Cross: an ancient instrument of torture.

Cross: in very bad humour.

Cross: a punch thrown across an opponent's punch.

1

'A cross is only agony if you are aware of it.'

Irish saying

It took them a time to crucify the kid. Not that he was giving them any trouble; in fact, he'd been almost co-operative. No, the problem was getting the nails into his palms – they kept hitting bone.

Meanwhile, the kid was muttering something.

The younger one said, 'Whimpering for his mother.'

The girl leaned close and said in a tone of surprise, 'He's praying.'

What was she expecting – a song?

The father lifted the hammer, said, 'It's going to be light soon.'

Sure enough, the first rays of dawn cutting across the small hill, throwing a splatter of light across the figure on the cross, looked almost like care.

'Why aren't you bloody dead?'

How to reply? I wanted to say, 'Tried my level best, really, I wanted to die. Surviving was not my plan, honestly.'

Malachy was my old arch enemy, my nemesis, and, like the best of ancient Irish adversaries, I'd even saved his arse once.

He was the heaviest smoker I'd ever met and God knows I've met me share. He now chain-lit another, growled, 'They shot the wrong fucker.'

Lovely language from a priest, right? But Malachy never followed any clerical rule I'd ever heard of. He meant Cody, a young kid who I saw as my surrogate son and who had taken the bullets meant for me. Even now, he lay in a coma and his chances of survival varied from real low to plain abysmal.

The shooting hadn't helped my limp, the result of a beating with a hurley. I was thus limping along the canal, seeing the ducks but not appreciating them as I once had. Nature no longer held any merit. Heard my name called and there was Father Malachy, the bane of my life. When I ended up trying to help him, was he grateful? Was he fuck. He had the most addictive personality I'd ever met, be it nicotine, cakes, tea or simply aggression, and addictive personalities are my forte. I've always wanted to say *my forte* – gives a hint of learning, but not showy with it. In truth, my forte was booze. He was looking grumpy, shabby and priestly. That is, furtive.

He had greeted me with that crack about being bloody dead and seemed downright angry. He was dressed in the clerical gear: black suit shiny from wear and the pants misshapen, shoes that looked like they'd given ten years' hard service. Dandruff lined his shoulders like a gentle fall of snow.

I said, 'Nice to see you too.' Let a sprinkle of granite leak over the words and kept my eyes fixed on him. He flicked the butt into the water, startling the ducks.

I added, 'Still concerned for the environment?'

His lip curling in distaste, he snapped, 'Is that sarcasm? Don't you try that stuff on me, boyo.'

The summer was nearly done. Already you could feel that hint of the Galway winter bite; soon the evenings would be getting dark earlier, and if I'd only known, darkness of a whole other hue was coming down the pike. But all I heard were the sounds of the college, just a tutorial away from where we stood. Galway is one of those cities where sound carries along the breeze like the faintest whisper of prayers you never said, muted but present.

I turned my attention afresh to Malachy. We were back to our old antagonism, business as usual.

Before I could reply he said, 'I gave the boy the last rites, did you know that? Anointed him with the oils. They thought he was a goner.'

I suppose gratitude was expected, but I went, 'Isn't that, like, your job, ministering to the sick, comforting the dying, stuff like that?'

He gave me the full appraisal, as if I'd somehow tricked him, said, 'You look like death warmed up.'

I turned to go, shot, 'That's a help.'

Fumbling for another cig, he asked, 'Did they find the shooter?'

Good question. Ni Iomaire – in English, Ridge, a female Guard, known as a Ban Gardai – had told me they'd ruled out one of the suspects, a stalker I'd leaned on. He was in Dublin on the day of the shooting. That left a woman, Kate Clare, sister of a suspected priest-killer. I didn't mention her to Ridge. It was complicated: I'd felt responsible for the death of her brother, and if she shot at me, I wasn't all that sure what the hell I wanted to do. She may also have killed others. I'd figured I'd deal with her when I regained my strength.

I said to Malachy, 'No, they ruled out the prime suspect.'

He wasn't satisfied with that. 'So, the person who shot your friend is still out there?'

I didn't want to discuss this, especially not with him, said, 'Not much escapes you.'

Then he abruptly changed tack. 'You ever visit your mother's grave?'

There are many crimes in the Irish lexicon, odd actions that in the UK wouldn't even rate a mention, but here were nigh on unforgivable.

Topping the list are:

Silence or reticence. You've got to be able to chat, preferably incessantly. Making sense isn't even part of the equation.

Not buying a round. You might think no one notices, but they do.

Having notions, ideas above your imagined station.

Neglecting the grave of your family.

There are others, such as having a posh accent, disliking hurling, watching BBC, but they are the second division. There's a way back from them, but the first division, you are fucked.

I tried, 'Believe it or not, when you're visiting a shot boy, shot full of bloody holes, it's harder than you might think to nip out to the cemetery.'

He blew that off, said, "Tis a thundering disgrace.'

The current national disgrace was the major hospitals admitting they'd been selling the body parts of dead children without the permission of the parents. Even the tax shenanigans of the country's politicians paled in comparison to this. The Government had pledged that *heads would roll* – translate as, scapegoats would be found. I'd had enough of Malachy and made to move away.

He asked, 'What do you make of the crucifixion?'

I was lost. Was this some metaphysical query? I went for the stock reply. 'I take it as an article of faith.'

Lame, right?

We'd been walking, walking and sparring, and had reached a shop at the top of the canal. Moved under the store's canopy as drops of rain began to fall.

A man emerged, stopped, pointed at a No Smoking decal, barked, 'Can't you read?'

Malachy rounded on him, went, 'Can't you mind your own business? Fuck off.'

As I said, not your expected religious reply.

The man hesitated then stomped away.

Malachy glared at me, then said, 'When the Prods crucified some poor hoor two years ago, I believed it was just one more variation on the punishment stuff that paramilitaries do, but I thought it was confined to the North.'

I tried for deep, said, 'Nothing is confined to the North.'

He was disgusted, began to walk away and said, 'You're

drinking again. Why did I think I could talk sensible to you?'

I watched him amble off, scratching his head, a cloud of light dandruff in his wake. It never occurred to me the horror he'd mentioned would have anything to do with me. Boy, was I wrong about that.

The booze, sure, I was *nearly* drinking again. You get shot at, you're going to have a lot of shots in the aftermath. Course you are. It's cast-iron justification. More and more, I'd begun to re-walk my city. What is it Bruce Springsteen titled his New York, 'My City Of Ruins'? At the back of my mind was the seed of escape, get the hell out, so I'd decided to see my town from the ground down. Ground zero.

I moved from the canal to St Joseph's Church, and a little along that road is what the locals now term Little Africa. A whole area of shops, apartments, businesses run by Nigerians, Ugandans, Zambesians, people from every part of the massive continent. To me, a white Irish Catholic, it was a staggering change, little black kids play-ing in the streets, drum beats echoing from open windows, and the women were beautiful. I saw dazzling shawls, scarves, dresses of every variety. And friendly . . . If you smiled at them, they responded with true warmth.

And that, despite the despicable graffiti on the walls:

Non Irish Not Welcome

Irish Nazis . . . a shame of epic proportion.

An elderly black man was moving along in front of me and I said, 'How you doing?'

He gave me a look of amazement, then his face lit up and he said, 'I be doing real good, mon. And you, brother, how you be doing?'

I ventured I was doing OK and fuck, it made me whole day. I moved on, a near smile on me own face. Hitting the top of Dominic Street, I turned left and strolled towards the Small Crane.

Isn't that a marvellous name? So evocative, and you just have to ask . . . is there a large crane?

No.

Then you hit the pink triangle. I shit thee not. In Galway. A gay ghetto. Me father would turn in his grave.

Me, I'm delighted.

Keep the city moving, keep it mixed, blended, and just maybe we'll stop killing our own selves over hundreds of years of so-called religious difference.

But I was getting too deep for me own liking, muttered, 'Bit late for you to be getting a social/political conscience.'

There's a lesbian bar on the corner and I would have loved me bigoted mother to know that. She'd have put a match to it and then got a Mass said.

I had quickened my pace, was on Quay Street, the Temple Bar of Galway, smaller but no less riotous, bastion of English hen parties and general mayhem, imported or otherwise. I turned at the flash hotel called Brennan's Yard, where the literati drank.

I had dreaded returning to my apartment. There's a Vince Gill song, 'I Never Knew Lonely'. You live on your own, see a loved one go down, there's few depressions like entering an empty apartment, the silent echoes mocking you. I wanted to roar, 'Honey, I'm home.'

I walked slowly up the stairs of my building, dread in my gut, the keys in my hand. There was a key ring attached, given to me by Cody, it had a Sherlock Holmes figurine. I took a deep breath, turned the key. I'd been to the off-licence, got my back-up.

Bottle of Jameson in my hand, I walked in, found a glass, poured a healthy measure, toasted, 'Welcome home, shithead.'

No matter what the cost – and I've paid as dear a price as there is – those first moments when the booze lights your world, there is nothing . . . nothing to touch that. Put the cap on the bottle. I was back to the goddamn longing, to trying to keep within a certain level of balance. Shite, I'd been down this road a thousand times, never worked, always ended in disaster. The silence in the room was deafening.

I'd been doing this demented stuff a while now, buying booze, pouring it and then pouring it down the toilet, each time muttering like a befuddled mantra, 'Down the toilet, like my life.'

Before the shooting – What a line that is, a real conversation spinner, beats *Where I took my vacation* hands down – I'd been trying to implement changes, had decided to change the things I could. Got as far as buying a whole new range of music, stuff I'd been reading about for years but never got round to hearing. Picked up a CD by Tom Russell, little realizing the serendipity of one track. The album was titled *Modern Art* and he had a recording of Bukowski's poem 'Crucifix In A Death Hand'.

I noticed I had the volume on full and wondered if me hearing was going. I poured the whiskey down the toilet. Once the drink compulsion eased, I looked round my home. Was there a single item that meant anything? The books were lined against the wall, a thin layer of dust on the spines. Like the shadows on my life, the dust had settled slowly and it didn't seem like anyone was going to eradicate it.

2

*'Men are so inevitably mad that not to be mad would be
to give a mad twist to madness.'*

Pascal, *Pensées*, 412

The girl was humming softly, an old Irish melody she no longer knew the name of. It was her mother's song and sometimes, if the girl turned real quick, she thought she could catch a glimpse of her mother, those blue eyes fixed on something in the distance, her slight figure, like a tiny ballerina, shimmering in the half light of the dying day.

She never told anyone of this, hugged it to herself like the softest fabric, like the piece of Irish linen her mother had put so much value on. It had been brought out on special occasions, handled with loving care and then put away, her mother saying in that soft Irish lilt, 'This will be yours some day, alannah.'

Alannah – my child – the first Irish word that held any real significance for her.

The girl's eyes moved around the room: cheap wallpaper was peeling from the top, a thin strip of carpet barely covered the floor and the windows badly needed to be cleaned. Her mother would never have allowed that, those windows would have been sparkling.

Near the door was the cross, a heavy hand-carved piece,

the features of the Christ outlining the torment, the nails clearly visible in the hands and feet. Her mind flashed to that other figure and she lingered on the image for a time. It was burned into her memory like a promise she'd made to her mother, and in her own way she had fulfilled the pledge. There was so much to do yet.

And then she smiled. The mantra her mother had used: 'So much to do.'

She was maybe six, and her mother had decided to give the house a total clean. 'Top to bottom.'

For some reason that had struck the child as hilarious, and as she laughed her mother had joined in, the two of them, arms round each other, laughing like they'd won the lottery.

When the laughter had subsided, her mother had looked right into her eyes, asked, 'Do you know how much I love you?'

And she'd said, to her mother's total delight, 'Top to bottom.'

The girl felt her eyes begin to fill with tears and she stood up abruptly, began to pace the worn carpet. She focused on what she had to do next, her conviction that not only would it be done but in such a way that it would scream, like the silent Christ on the hand-carved cross.

She resumed her humming as the details began to take shape.

3

'You put the heart crossways in me.'

Irish expression for being given a bad fright.

There's an open-plan café in the Eyre Square shopping centre.

Eyre Square was still in the throes of a major re-development and, like everything else, was two years behind completion. En route to the centre, I'd stopped for a moment by the site of Brown's Doorway which, like the statue of Padraig O'Conaire, had been removed. They'd promised they'd restore them and there were maybe three people in the city who actually believed it. There'd once been a monument to Lord Clanricarde in Eyre Square. Like a metaphor for all our history, it had been paid for by his tenants and, need I add, against their will. My father had told me of the wild celebrations in 1922 when it had been taken down, and, nice touch, after they hammered it to smithereens they used the base for the statue of O'Conaire.

You look straight down the Square and there's the Great Southern Hotel, though what was so great about it was anyone's guess. It was expensive, but then, wasn't every-thing? According to a recent poll, it was cheaper to live in

New York. When I was a child, two cannons had stood sentry right where I stood and the whole park had been circled by railings. They were long gone.

As were the fairs.

Fair day in Galway meant fair day in Eyre Square. These affairs began around four a.m. Get at it early.

And they did.

Cattle, sheep, pigs and horses were paraded with varying degrees of pride and cunning. The real winners were the pubs which sprang up to cater for the crowd. And of course along came a bank – Bank of Ireland, to my back, had now a massive building, begun no doubt in those better times.

Deals were still made on Eyre Square but they involved dope, women, passports and, naturally, booze.

I sighed for a loss too profound for articulation and turned, walked past Faller's the jeweller's and crossed the road into the centre proper. Took the down escalator, in every sense, and went to the café on the lower floor.

You sit, have a snack, watch the tourists. Scarce this year, due to fear of flying, terrorists, rising prices. All the retail outlets had S A L E signs in the windows, a sure sign of desperation and an economy on the slide. Our Celtic Tiger had roared and loud for nigh on eight years and man, we wallowed in its trough. Now the downside, we didn't feed that goddamn animal and the whore died.

Got me a latte, a slice of Danish I hadn't touched and the *Irish Independent*. We'd done woesome at the Olympics, maybe the worst ever. Our best and our brightest, Sonia O'Sullivan, had trailed in last. You want to see the difference between the good old USA and us . . . one of our athletes came eleventh, we were delighted as he'd achieved a *personal best*. The American swimmer currently on his fourth Gold was depressed as he wasn't going to emulate the achievement of Mark Spitz. At the very beginning of the Games, the Irish team had been rocked by a dope scandal. The guilty party said he hoped to work with anti-doping boards when his two-year ban was up. And we applauded him. Fuck, was it just me or was the country getting crazier? Religion, however heavy its hand, had for centuries provided a ballast against despair. Mired in more and more disgrace, the people no longer had much faith in the clergy providing anything other than tabloid fodder. It probably explained why every new-fangled cult had managed to find a congregation in the city. Even the Scientologists had an office. We were expecting Tom Cruise any day.

It was only a few years since I'd been a regular church-goer, the priest even called me by my first name, but the Magdalen Laundry's revelations stopped me cold, and a black leather coat I'd brought back from London had been stolen during Mass and I wouldn't swear to it but I saw a priest wearing one very similar.

The newspapers were screaming about a crucifixion, but I skipped that, moved to the more mundane stuff. I sipped my coffee, read about the furore at the Black Box, a venue on the dyke road – a simulated lesbian performance had outraged residents. Further along the way, in Bohermore, a shop selling sex items had to close due to pickets. The proprietor sneered, 'They thought we were having sex in the shop.' He added that the huge publicity had ensured the success of his new premises in the city centre.

I reached for my cigarettes, then realized I didn't smoke any more. And even if I did, you weren't allowed to smoke in the area. The Irish, despite all expectations, had gone along with the new law without a murmur. Had we lost our balls?

You betcha.

I threw the paper aside. A young man with long, dank hair sat opposite me. He'd a can of Red Bull. There was no real physical resemblance to Cody, but he reminded me of him and that was a hurt as harsh as the black coffee I wished I'd ordered.

He reminded me too of Joey Ramone. He slurped from the can and I mean *slurped* – among the most annoying sounds at the best of times, but with a very bad mood almost unbearable. I wanted to reach over, slap his face, roar *Have some fucking finesse*. Reined it in, finished the latte and considered a double espresso. The kid was looking at me. Was it myself or was he smirking?

I stared at him, asked, 'I know you?' Let a dribble of edge in there.

He drained the can, began to crush it, bending it out of shape, flicked long strands of hair out of his eyes, answered, 'Sorry sir, I was miles away.'

Lots of attitude in the *sir*.

A radio was playing in one of the shops and I heard Morrissey with his current hit, 'First Of The Gang To Die'. Gives me a shiver, something prophetic in that. The kid was staring at a scar on my face, the result of a bad beating from two brothers who were not fond of the tinkers.

'That from a knife?'

I touched the spot. I was still attempting to get used to the odd fact that my voice had altered since I stopped smoking, like I've smoked a million cigs, washed over with rotgut, less husky than fucked. I sort of admired his cheek and went, 'How would you know that? You in the army?'

Not that I thought for a moment he was. He was too fragile.

He grinned, answered, 'No, just London.'

He was scratching his arms. I recognized the speed burn, and then he started to talk, a spew of words, his mouth unable to keep up with the flow of thought. 'You ever listen to The Libertines? Pete Doherty, their singer, is like, gone from dope, and The Black Keys, 10 AM Automatic, fatback blues and I've gotta get me some Prodigy. Dunst, he's living the dream, man, and you ever get to London, you gotta hear Roots Manuva, he's like –'

He paused, losing the thread, then, 'Razor rap and funny, you know?'

Stopped, realizing he'd given me a mini lecture on music, just like Cody used to do, without me ever mentioning it.

So I cut him some slack, said, 'You like music, kid?'

His attention span was so like Cody's. One minute he was focused on you, then, bang, he was off again, as if one thought, one line of concentration was too much. He stood up. 'See you around.'

Then he paused, added, 'Dude.'

The movie *Wayne's World* has a lot to answer for. It was one of Cody's favourites. I had no reply to this – not then, not now. I simply nodded and he shambled off, in that half crouch young people adopt, like, who gives a fuck?

A waitress began clearing the table. She held the bent Red Bull tin, pissed by it, indicated my slice of Danish. 'You going to eat that?'

I looked at her and asked, 'You like The Prodigy?'

I had a mobile phone. Not that it ever rang, but it made me feel vaguely connected so I dutifully charged it daily. Carried it like a sad prayer in my jacket.

Went to McSwiggan's. There's a tree in the centre of the pub, always reassures me that the country still has a sense of the absurd.

It's situated in Wood Quay, not a spit away from Hidden Valley, where I once briefly had a home, courtesy of the tinkers. Wood Quay is one of the few real neighbourhoods in Galway. The people have lived there for generations and managed to hold on to their homes despite the rampant developers. You stand at the bottom of Eyre Street and you can see the whole of the area, the park that is still green, still untouched, where the kids play hurling and, OK, frisbee, but hurling has the upper, for the moment, and just beyond it is Lough Corrib. It gives a sense of community and they have their own street carnival every year. They are fiercely proud of how they've managed to stay intact in a city of so many rapid and ruthless changes.

McSwiggan's is right at the beginning of the neighbourhood. A newish pub, it has somehow grabbed an echo of old Galway. The tree is right in at the back and yes, they

built the pub round it. Now that to me is called having
your priorities correct. And more of a rarity, the staff are
all Irish. This is becoming more and more of an oddity.

It was just after twelve and the bar guy was doing pub
stuff, a frenzy of glass-polishing, stocking shelves, but
cheerful with it.

'Howyah?'

I acknowledged I was OK, ordered a pint and a small
Jameson.

'Ice with that?'

I gave him the look. Was he serious?

He said, 'No ice it is.'

The pub smelled odd and he noticed me noticing, said,
'It's the lack of nicotine.'

Christ, he was right.

Then he added, 'Our showjumper got a gold medal.'

I was delighted. I don't know shit from horses, but a
gold, the country would be on the piss for a month.

He let my pint sit before he creamed off the head – knew
his stuff – and put the Jameson on the counter. 'I've a ticket
for the Madonna concert.'

Almost like the old Ireland, telling you their business
without you ever asking. I took a smell of the Jameson and
instantly I was convivial.

'You're a fan, right?'

Not the brightest query seeing as he'd a ticket, but
luckily logic counts for very little in such exchanges. He
was horrified.

'Don't be fecking mad, I hate the cow.'

I managed to keep the drink on the table, not to drink it.

You have to think, *What dementia, ordering booze and not drinking?*

I know just how mad it was. But it kept me sober, if far from sane.

I thought of Cody, lying in the coma, and of Kate Clare too, the woman who killed the priest and was now my prime suspect for shooting Cody. I knew I should be devoting more energy to finding her or whoever did the shooting but I couldn't get past Cody and his condition. He'd been the surrogate son I'd never dreamed I'd have, then just when we bonded, when I'd actually begun to think of him as family, he'd been snatched from me.

A vengeful God?

He certainly had it in for me. Every time I seemed to get up off me knees, He wiped the fucking floor with me. Did I believe in Him? You betcha, and it was real personal. I'd mutter in the mornings, *Do Your worst and let's see how I take it*. A hollow taunt in the face of chaos, bravado in place of faith. I shook my head to clear it of God and His spite, stood, figured it was time to head.

Leaving, I said to the bar guy, my untouched drinks sitting like forlorn friends, 'Hope the concert goes well.'

He paused, mid-glass-cleaning, gaped at me, said, 'I'm praying for rain.'

In Ireland you don't have to pray too fervently for that.

4

'A crucified without a cross.'

Description of the saint Padre Pio by the faithful.

When I was first visiting Cody in the hospital, I was waylaid one afternoon by a man. He had that pious look beloved of priests and do-gooders.

He said, 'Are we feeling better?'

I was not a very good hospital visitor, not one of those cheery stoic folk who enrich your day when you encounter them. I was bad tempered, hurt and dying for a drink. I stared at him. 'I don't know about you, pal, and truth to tell I don't care, but I'm feeling like shite.'

He nodded, could deal with aggression, in fact looked like he expected it. He was not going to be disappointed. He leaned closer, said, 'Anger is good. Get that bad vibe out there. Don't hold it in.'

We were in the corridor outside Cody's room and, as always, I was bracing myself to enter, so the diversion wasn't unwelcome. I started to walk away, glad of the reprieve, and he followed as I knew he would.

We reached what is called the *long ward*, open planning if you will. Row on row of beds, no privacy. I'd occupied more than my share of them.

'Where did you learn that crap? I mean, at home, when you're sitting in front of the telly, do you seriously talk like that? Jeez, I mean, come on.'

More smiles. I was obviously the dream he nurtured.

I asked, 'And who the hell are you, apart from a monumental pain in the ass?'

He did a thing with his eyes that was meant to convey compassion and – what's the buzz word? – yeah, empathy. Made him look shifty. Would you buy a used car from this guy?

Nope.

He was cooking now, said, 'See me as a non-judgemental friend.'

Like that was going to happen.

I said, 'You want to be my friend, you could do me a favour. How would that be, as a sign of our closeness?'

Slight cloud over his cheerful face, he asked, 'Erm, OK, what would that be?'

'Hop over the road to the Riverside Inn, grab me a bottle of Jameson.'

He sighed, leaned back, as if this was the very thing he knew he'd hear, let out a long breath. 'Ah, herein is the crux of the matter.'

Crux.

Is there a class in these guys' training, say day three, when they're given a booklet containing all the words they can use that no one else does, which they can just lob into the conversation, kill it stone dead.

I'd stopped at the end of the long ward. The very last bed was empty and that meant only one thing: the patient had died. They keep that bed for the ones who aren't going to make it so they can whisk them out of there in jig time, without disturbing the other patients. I stared at that empty bed, a myriad of dread in my gut.

When I didn't respond, he added, 'Alcohol seems to have been a major part in your . . .'

He selected the next word like a spinster eyeing a box of her favourite chocolates: didn't go with *downfall*, though he considered it, opted for the less dangerous '. . . trouble.'

I asked, 'You want to hear about my life when I was sober, when I wasn't drinking, you want to know about the success that was?'

He shifted his weight, suspecting this was not going to be pleasant.

'If you wish to share.'

I got right up in his face. He'd have backed off 'cept he was up against the death bed.

I said, 'Yeah, I was sober, hadn't had a drink in months, and guess what? I got a little girl killed. Three years old, the most beautiful child you ever saw, a fucking dote, and there's me, not drinking, minding her, she goes out a top-floor window. And her parents, my best friends, how do you think they felt about me being sober then?'

He didn't have a platitude but tried, 'Life is no bowl of cherries and sometimes terrible things happen. We must move on, not let events sour us.'

I stopped, stared at him, near shouted, 'No bowl of fucking cherries? You're unbelievable. If I ever run into the child's parents, I'll mention the goddamn cherries, I'm sure that will really ease their grief.'

I was seething, had to move, so I eased up on the physical crowding I'd been doing, let him loose, and began to move out towards the nurses' station. He was following behind me.

I said, 'Listen – you listening? – I'm going for a piss. You come in behind me and I'll kick you in the balls. That facing my anger? That real enough?'

But these guys, you're talking to a granite wall. He looked like he was going to extend his arms, maybe embrace me, and that would have been such a mistake.

He tried, 'Jack, Jack, I'm reaching out to you. Do you really want to keep making the same tragic choices?'

Turning to go into the toilet, I asked, 'You familiar with Dudley Moore?'

He sensed a trap, ventured, 'Erm, yes.'

I looked round as if I was going to take him into my confidence, said, 'Dudley Moore was interviewing his great friend Peter Cook, asked him if he'd learned from his mistakes, and Cook replied, "Yes, absolutely, I can repeat them almost perfectly."'

In the bathroom, a man trailing an IV was trying to have a pee. He looked at me and said, 'What a way for a grown man to end up.'

I had no argument there.

That encounter with the zealot was replaying in my mind as I strolled along Shop Street. When I'd left my flat I'd been in a reasonable state of mind, but this flashback was bringing me down and fast.

Summer was definitely over. That peculiar light, unique

to the West of Ireland, was flooding the street – it's a blend of brightness but always with that threat of rain, and it glistens like wet crystal even as it soothes you. The edge of darkness is creeping along the horizon and you get the feeling you'd better grab it while it lasts.

Outside Eason's Bookshop, a group of Christians were singing a rock version of 'One Day At A Time'. They had the well-scrubbed faces of clean-living young people. A girl in her late teens detached herself from the group when she noticed my interest, pushed a batch of leaflets at me and said, 'Jesus loves you.'

I don't know why but my mood was lifting: I was en route to the pub, the light was giving its last burst of spectacular clarity. But she annoyed me and I snapped, 'How do you know?'

Took her aback, but the training kicked in and she produced the requisite dead smile with a well-rehearsed slogan.

'Through music, we are making Christianity better.'

Same tired old shit with a shiny gloss. A few days back I'd watched *King of the Hill*, an episode where Hank confronted a set of trendy born-agains. Their combination of evangelism and tattoos really pissed him off. I faced the girl now and used the line Hank had retaliated with.

'You people aren't making Christianity better, you're making rock 'n' roll worse.'

Didn't faze her. Using her index fingers she made the sign of the cross, like you would to ward off a vampire, and muttered some incantation. I moved on, the sound of their singing like an assault on my ears. Right beside

Eason's, almost, is Garavan's, one of the old pubs, still not yet modernized. Books and booze, neighbours of our heritage.

The barman saw the leaflets in my hand, Jesus in large red letters on the front.

'They convert you?'

I leaned on the counter. 'Take a wild flogging guess.'

He began to build my pint of black, reached behind for a shot of Jameson, his movements a fluid action, no break in the sequence, all the more impressive as I hadn't asked for either. He said, 'Believe it or not, they're good for business. People hear them, think, *Christ, I need a drink.*'

I didn't inquire as to how he knew my order. I was afraid he'd tell me.

The smallest event can sometimes trigger a whole set of actions and as I got my hand on the glass, I saw the girl's sign of the cross and remembered the crucifixion. Ridge was on my mind, too. In the most bizarre way, I loved her – fuck, not that I'd ever admit that, ever. She irritated me to the ninth level of hell and beyond, but what else is love but all that and still hanging in there? Her being gay only added to the conundrum. Ah, I was a mess. And Cody, wasn't he a victim of some cold bastard? Some ruthless whore who just took him out. That girl had cursed me and opened yet again the road to devastation, but it was the road I travelled most.

I took my drinks and moved over to the snug, a small cubbyhole designed to give you if not peace then a degree of privacy. The pint of Guinness was a work of art. Perfectly poured, the head a precise slice of cream. Seemed almost a shame not to drink it. Malcolm Lowry's *Under the Volcano* came unsought into my mind. If I'd only had a little foresight – the last lines of that terrifying book, they throw a dead dog into the grave, on top of the dead consul. I didn't see any connecting lines and what an irony be there.

You sit behind a pint like that, a pure gift, with the Jameson already weaving its dark magic on your eyes, you can believe that Iraq is indeed on the other side of the world, that winter isn't coming, that the Galway light will always hold that beautiful fascination and that priests are our protectors, not predators. You won't have the illusion for very long, but the moment is priceless.

I didn't have any more hope in religion, so I took worship at whatever altar provided brief solace. Of course, like the best shot at heaven, it was surrounded by hell on every border. Then I chided my own self, muttered *enough with the deep shit, it's just a bloody drink*, and I'd raised the glass when a man peered round the partition.

'Jack Taylor?'

I might actually have drank that time. This was my Russian roulette, Irish style. Each time I ordered a drink, I never knew if I'd actually swallow it, but I was fairly sure I would do soon, and deep down I hoped so. I looked at the man who had spoken my name with familiarity.

I was tempted to deny it. No good ever came of these inquiries. I didn't hide my annoyance.

'Yeah?'

He was big – over six foot – in his early sixties, with a weather-beaten face, a bald head and nervous eyes. Wearing a very fine suit and solid heavy-duty shoes, he said, 'I'm sorry to disturb you, but I've been looking for you for quite a few days.' A slight testiness in his tone, as if he had better things to do than search for me.

I touched the pint. It felt good, if a little soured by the interruption.

'So you've found me. What's your problem?' I didn't make any attempt to disguise my irritation.

He put his hand out. 'I'm Edward O'Brien.'

I ignored his hand, asked, 'And that's supposed to mean something? Tell you, pal, it don't mean shit to me.'

He gave an almost knowing smile. 'They told me you'd a sharp tongue but a good heart.'

Before I could respond to this piece of nonsense, he said, 'I need your help.'

More to get rid of him than out of interest, I asked, 'For what?'

'To find my dog.'

I nearly laughed. Here I was, fixing to find who crucified a man, and this lunatic lost his dog?

'You're fucking kidding, someone put you up to this, it's like some kind of lame joke.'

He was shocked. His face registering hurt, he said, 'I love that little guy.'

I shook my head, waved him away.

He didn't go, continued, 'I'm a professor at the university and I represent the residents of Newcastle. Are you at all *au fait* with the area?'

Au fait!

And being a professor, like that was going to cut some ice with me. The last professor I encountered had been a murdering bastard. I near shouted, 'Yo, Prof, I'm from Galway, I know where the bloody place is.'

He ploughed on.

'Five homes have had their dogs stolen. We heard you were good at finding things, and we'll pay you.'

When I didn't leap at the opportunity, he added, 'And pay well.'

The temptation to go *Doggone* was ferocious.

I said, 'Leave it with me, I'll see what I can do.'

He straightened up. 'Thank you so much. It means an awful lot to us.'

He was on his way when I said, 'They were wrong, what they told you about me.'

His face brightened. 'That you had a sharp tongue?'

'No, that I had a good heart.'

5

Cross-eyed.

Back in my apartment, I was preparing for my siesta. I had my own version of this deal: try to get some food down, half a painkiller/tranquillizer and sayonara suckers. Pulled on a long T-shirt with the logo THE JAMES DEANS, brushed my teeth and had a brief look at Sky News. Maybe the world had improved.

It hadn't.

The Republican Convention was taking place in New York. Christopher Hitchens had written that it was going to be a tight race and I believed him. Chechen rebels had seized a school and were threatening to kill three hundred kids if their fighters weren't released. One of the little girls was dragged to safety and I swear, she was the spit of Serena May. Part of the whole mountain of guilt, remorse, was that every little girl reminded me of her. How could they not?

I switched off fast, swallowed the medication and waited for it to meld into the blood, muttering, 'God, I know you've fucked me good and probably for all time, but hey, cut me a bit of slack – no dreams of the child, or you know what? I'll drink again.'

Yeah, threatening God, real smart idea, like He gave a toss in the first place. But what the hell.

I added as a rider, 'Didn't I help a priest, doesn't that count?'

Probably not.

A knock on the door.

'Fuck.'

Could I risk ignoring it? Sleep was already creeping along my nerves. More knocking and I sighed, opened it.

Ridge.

She was in uniform, looking serious, intimidating.

I said, 'I paid my television licence, officer.'

She was not amused, but then, she rarely was. Our relationship was usually combative, aggressive, and however much we tried, we never could get free of each other. Before Cody had been shot, we'd reached a sort of warmth. She was in a relationship and it appeared we might establish some sort of friendship.

I'd saved her from a very vicious stalker and I knew how much she appreciated it, but she reacted with hostility to being indebted, and God knows, no one understood this better than me. You help me out, I feel like I owe you, and till the sheet is clean I'm uneasy, jumpy, and what I know best is antagonism. The terrible truth, and we both knew it, was we needed to be linked, *were* linked, and somewhere in all that mess we were both scared we'd lose each other.

Is this fucked up? Sure. Or maybe it's just pure Irish.

I often thought, if only she weren't gay, would there be something?

If I wasn't an alcoholic. If . . . if . . . if.

Back through the years, we'd helped each other more than anyone else. Then we'd reach a plateau of near intimacy and one or both of us would scuttle for cover. Wouldn't it break your heart. It certainly broke mine, and as for Ridge, a smashed heart was written on her face if you could get past the front.

But the shooting had changed everything. My bitterness was not going to bring back the vague thread of closeness we'd been near.

She accused, 'You're only getting up?'

Her face was devoid of make-up and she looked strained.

'Actually, I was going to bed.'

She made a show of checking her watch. 'It's one thirty in the afternoon.'

I was tempted to slam the door in her face, shout, *Aw, fuck off,* but went with 'You came round to tell me the time? I have a watch.'

She brushed past me and marched into the sitting room.

I closed the door, said, 'It's not going to endear me to the neighbours, having Guards at the door.'

She looked round, not seeing anything to improve her mood, so I asked, 'You want something? A beer, a large whiskey?'

Needling her.

She said, 'I'd have thought jokes about alcoholism were hardly appropriate.'

We stood, hostility swirling round us till I asked, 'What, you came round, figured you'd just bust my balls? Things a bit slow on the traffic front?'

The wind seemed to go out of her. She slumped in a chair, asked, 'You know how hard it is, being a Guard?'

I wanted to shout, *Hello, I used to be one*, but said nothing.

She continued, 'And being a woman – a gay woman – they love that. You just know you're not on any promotion list. Last year they issued us with skirts to soften our image, like a thug is going to appreciate the difference, drop his knife and say, "Sorry, didn't realize you were wearing a skirt." None of the other women wear them. I have my baton, a utility belt that takes the handcuffs, has a pouch for the radio, a face shield for mouth-to-mouth resuscitation and latex gloves for health and safety, especially when you have to search a body.'

She gave a small shudder as she said this, then added, 'They allow make-up, did you know that? As long as it's not red lipstick or blatant. Our hair has to be a certain length. There's a bitch, my sergeant, she measures my hair, so I started to wear a ponytail and she said it had to go under my cap.'

It was like she'd never really allowed herself to examine the details of her job and I wondered where this was going. She wasn't finished.

'We're supposed to take turns in the patrol car and that's always in pairs. On the beat, you're often on your own. You know how many times I've got to ride in the car?'

I had to say something so tried, 'Not often, I'd guess.'

'Never. Is that fair? But what am I saying? Fair isn't the deal. I get stuck in the station a lot. I hate that, it's like being in an office, people looking for driving licences, passports or reporting thefts. It's so boring. Then they bring in a drunk, a lot of drunks . . .'

She eyed me. I was obviously in that category.

I was tempted to mock, *Ah, poor little Ridge, they won't let you ride in the big car.*

But I held back and she went on, 'The thing is, I love being a Guard, but if I don't get promoted soon, I'll have to consider resigning.'

Her face as she said this was a tragedy in miniature. Sleep was trying to claim me and I wanted her to fuck off, so I said, 'Do whatever you have to do to get the promotion.'

She looked right at me and I realized we'd come to the whole point of the visit.

She said, 'I'm very worried about a health problem and I don't know who to tell.'

Sometimes simplicity is the only route, so I said, 'Tell me.'

She took a deep breath.

'I found a lump on my breast. It might be just tissue, but –'

I didn't hesitate.

'You have to get it checked.'

She was lost for a moment, imagining, who knows, what horrible implications.

I pressed on. 'Ridge, promise me you'll make an appointment.'

She re-focused.

'OK, I will, but there is something else.'

I waited. She asked, 'You know about the crucifixion?'

I nodded, even though I knew precious little.

She said, 'He was eighteen years of age, John Willis, they

nailed him to the cross and mounted the thing on the hill above the city dump. We thought maybe it was a drug deal, a warning to others, or maybe even political. It isn't. He comes from a respectable family, was due to start college and has no record.'

She waited for my input.

I was stunned, shocked, sickened. Visions of Cody were in my head and I thought I might throw up. Took me a solid five minutes before I could gasp, 'Any leads?'

She composed herself, curbing the excitement the case stirred in her. 'We have nothing – no leads, nothing to go on, it's dead in the water. But if a person were able to shed any light on it, it would be a career-maker.'

It took me a moment to grasp.

'Ah no, you want me to nose around. You're the one always telling me to get out of this whole sordid game, that it will destroy me.'

She at least had the grace to seem ashamed, then said, 'I don't want you to do anything dangerous, but you have an uncanny knack for finding threads.'

Before I could refuse – and refuse I intended – she took out a sheet of paper and said, 'Here's the name, he lived in Claddagh, I'll leave it here. Just think about it, OK? That's all I ask, Jack.'

Jack.

She never used my first name. It was a measure of her desperation.

As she was heading for the door she said, 'You look beat, get some rest.'

With all the sarcasm I could muster, I said, 'I'm touched

by your concern. The next time I see you, I want to hear you've been for that check-up.' I tried to keep my tone light, not show how worried I was.

She was in the hall, a ray of light catching the gold buttons on her tunic. Looking almost impressive and vulnerable, she said, 'I'm not concerned, I was just trying to be polite.'

I shouted after her, 'Try harder.'

I slammed the door, letting the neighbours know I was back and with ferocity. Picked up the piece of paper, read:

> John Willis
> 3, Claddagh Park
> Galway

I sat in the chair, and before I could even begin to think about it, my eyes closed and sleep grabbed me.

Herbert Spencer wrote: 'There is a principle which is a bar against all information, which is proof against all arguments and which cannot fail to keep a man in everlasting ignorance – that principle is contempt prior to investigation.'

I, of course, have no idea what Spencer looked like, but in my addled sleep he appeared, carrying a hammer and nails and quoting the above, and then began shouting that this was not going to be solved as I was not in the right frame of mind. He looked a bit like my father and then roared, in Irish, '*Bhi curamach!*'

Be careful.

Ridge was in the dream too, but her part is lost to me, save she was extremely unhappy. Serena May, the dead child, of course appeared, her sad eyes locked on me till I woke, whimpering, drenched in sweat.

My apartment was dark, and I fumbled to see my watch . . . Jesus, seven o'clock, I'd been out for five hours. Resolved I'd cut way down on the sleepers. I made no such resolution regarding the bitterness – that was the only fuel I had.

6

'Sed libera nos a malo.'
'Deliver us from evil.'

The Lord's Prayer

The girl remembered the green walls of the mental hospital – puke green. She'd come to in a hospital bed and panic had hit first before she'd realized she was still alive. She hadn't known if she was relieved or not.

Then she'd seen her father, sitting on the hard chair by her bed, keeping vigil. His head had fallen forward and a slight dribble leaked from his mouth, making him look old. The crown of his head revealed a bald spot, still barely noticeable, but the loss had begun. His whole posture spoke of defeat. She'd known him through his many moods – angry, frustrated, grief stricken – but never, never had he surrendered.

If she stirred, she knew he'd wake, and she needed some time before that happened. She lay perfectly still, her mouth dry, her body feeling weak. But something had changed. She could sense a dark energy above her, waiting to be summoned. Those days after the tragedy, when she'd been inconsolable, she'd begun to lose her mind. She kept replaying how her mother must have felt, those moments before the close. And alone – her mother would have hated that.

The girl had hoarded a stash of her mother's sleeping pills, and on the street she scored a whole batch of other stuff. She had sat in her room, the pills in line, like tiny soldiers waiting for her orders. She liked the colours of them, lots of yellow, red and blue – blue, her mother's best loved shade. Walking point on those items of relief was the bottle of vodka. She took a deep swig, then . . . eeney, meeny, miney . . . let's have a blue, then a red . . . and why not two yellow, another tot of vodka. She felt the raw alcohol light up her stomach, the voice in her head asking, 'Are you going to kill yourself?'

And the other voice, still in its infancy – the dark one – answering, 'I just want the pain to stop.'

That all-encompassing grief had made her howl in silent anguish, her head tilted back, her mouth wide open but forming no sound, like a mute hyena. Her brother had come upon her thus and, frightened, he'd backed away, unable or unwilling to try and give her solace. The girl's voice, the voice of her childhood, attempting one last rally as she popped three red ones – such pretty colours – more alcohol, that young voice saying, 'Suicide is eternal damnation.'

The dark tone spitting back, 'And this, this . . . the way I am, a quivering mess of grief and anguish . . . is this not pure damnation?'

She didn't remember anything after that, only the dark voice sneering, 'We rule now.'

Wherever she'd been, that empty place between life and death had been where the transference had begun. The darkness had grown stronger, eroding the old her. She'd let out a deep breath, as if expelling the last remnants of the girl she'd been and, she thought with utter contempt, the weakling she'd been.

No more.

Let the shadows rule. Bring on the spectre of retribution and ferocious revenge.

It was then she'd noticed, out of her peripheral vision, flames beginning to build in the corner of the room, though when she looked directly there was nothing there. She'd let out a squeal of pure delight.

The sound had woken her father. He'd sat up suddenly, alarm on his face and then relief as he realized she was back.

If he'd only known.

He'd taken her slight hand in his own huge fists and squeezed it, saying, 'Tell me, baby, tell me what I can do to help.'

She'd sat up, a strength she'd never had before infusing her, and told him exactly what she wanted. With a delicious sense of power, she'd seen the horror on his face at what she proposed. The clarity of her thinking, shrouded in this new darkness, had been exhilarating.

He'd agreed with all her plans, though she could plainly see he was repulsed at the biblical scope of her vision. But he'd been so relieved to have her back, he'd have agreed to anything.

After he'd left, she'd curled up in a warm posture of total renewal, smiling at how happy he'd been that she hadn't died. Her smile had grown in malevolence as she wondered how he'd feel if he knew precisely who it was that had returned. A soothing weariness began to claim her, and before sleep took her she recalled her mother's description of the Church that was such a vital part of her life.

She'd said, 'Alannah, our Church is all we have. Our Lord Jesus Christ will not be mocked. He will smite those who damage his flock.'

Her mother had been among the finest members of the flock and the girl muttered, almost asleep, a smell of smoke in her nostrils, 'Behold a pale rider, trailing death and vengeance in his wake.'

The words were like black communion in her mouth.

7

*In Ireland, among the older generation,
it is believed that a prayer said at the foot
of the cross is always answered.*

I had to go to the hospital the next morning for my daily check on Cody, to see that the wounds were healing and he wasn't getting bedsores. Involved a two-hour wait. The news was on. The siege at the Russian school had ended in horror, disaster. Three hundred feared dead, most of them children, scenes of them fleeing in their underwear as the terrorists fired at them. I had to move away, heard the gasps of shock from the people in the waiting room. Then a report on Iraq: since the 'peace', *one thousand* American soldiers had died. When the nurse called me I was relieved to get away from the television.

The doctor, cheery, asked, 'How are you feeling?'

Multiple-choice answers:

Horrified

Depressed

Hungover

Like a bastard.

Said, 'Could be worse.'

We moved to Cody's bed, he looked . . . dead, tubes

everywhere, only a slight lifting of his chest indicating any life.

Whatever the hell that meant.

He did a full examination, going *Mmm* and tut-tutting, all guaranteed to put the heart crossways in you. Finally he was done and made some notes on a chart, then, 'He's healing well.'

A *but* hung in the air and I waited. I wasn't volunteering anything. Whatever he thought, he'd get to it, they always do, no point in adding to the sheet.

He sighed. 'His body has been subjected to an inordinate amount of . . .'

He was searching for a description so to cut to the chase I prompted, 'Punishment?'

I'd been beaten more times than I could count – with a hurley, an iron bar, fists, boots, and always with intent, so you could say I knew about that item. The shooting was like my Oscar, my highest pinnacle, all the others just building to the main event. The only slight deviation being, I wasn't the one who'd been shot.

Throw in the hammering from alcohol and you had the obituary card near complete. I'd picked the right word.

'Precisely.'

I figured we were done and got ready to leave.

He said, 'Alcohol is not conducive to the healing process.'

I tried, 'I don't think the kid is going to be hopping out for a pint any time soon, do you?'

He scowled – good word, that, a testament to my self-learning, fat fucking lot of good it did me – and snapped,

'Sarcasm is not really warranted. I didn't put the poor boy here and I'm doing my very best for him.'

Yada yada.

I wanted to shout, 'Do frigging better.'

He asked, 'Do you talk to him?'

'What?'

'We don't know for certain, but it's been shown that talking to a comatose victim helps the visitor, if nothing else, and who can say? Maybe he can hear you.'

What a load of bollocks.

I asked, 'What do you suggest – the football results, how Man U are faring, that Giggs is playing out of his skin? You think that might snap Cody out of the coma?'

God, I was so angry, a rage that threatened to engulf me.

The doctor caught it, said, 'You'll know best.' And strode off.

I know it was unfair, but as they say, he was there and an easy target. Part of me wanted to call him back, apologize, but nope, didn't do it.

When I got outside, I breathed a sigh of relief and muttered my old familiar mantra: 'This calls for a drink.'

I looked up at the darkening sky – summer was definitely done – and muttered to the God I no longer trusted, 'Couldn't I just have one day on the piss, and not have a hangover?'

I already knew the answer, but sometimes you pose the question just to keep your own self well and truly vexed.

8

The stations of the cross.

I was reading – trying to read – Bukowski, *South of No North*. My mind was going in a hundred directions, none of them good. Willed myself to concentrate, but couldn't do it. My mind filled with dread about Ridge and breast cancer, and Cody in the coma, was I going to settle down and read?

Yeah, like that was going to fly.

Put the book aside. This was not the best territory for me to be travelling. Checked my watch – thirty minutes to pub time. Somehow, I was holding it vaguely together, boozewise, though the urge to lash out was edging closer. The radio was on, playing tracks from Elvis Costello's new album *The Delivery Man*, which had a crazed duet with Lucinda Williams and a riot of guitars blowing rough alongside, then 'Heart Shaped Bruise' with my long-time favourite, Emmylou Harris. All you need to know is in the title, kicked the tattered remnants of any longing I still clung to. I stood, turned it off. My hearing was definitely on the blink. I could only do so much anguish before I went searching for a rope.

Looked out the window: a minor storm building, as
America was being battered by the third hurricane in three
weeks. This one, aptly called Ivan, was heading for New
Orleans and I was heading for the pub. Storms of my own.
Pulled on my all-weather Garda coat, item 8234. They still
wrote me letters attempting to get it back.

Dream on, fuckers.

A slight perspiration on my brow as I walked down by
Eyre Square. And for the sheer joy of it, I walked to
Eglington Street. It's about fifteen minutes from my flat. I
cut across the back of Eyre Square and came to it from the
west end. The Lions Tower, known as the Bastion, used to
be here and then became the site of the Garda barracks.

You can turn into Francis Street from there, and they
have the best greengrocer's in the city. You can buy seaweed there, known as Crannog, supposed to cure all ails.
I'd once tried it for a hangover and was as sick as forty
dogs, but I can't really blame the seaweed. Americans were
intrigued by this 'commodity' and were never quite sure if
we were serious.

Me neither. I think it belongs on the beach, washed up
and abandoned.

The Sisters of Mercy had a school here and my mother
and Nora Barnacle attended, though not, of course, at the
same time. To hear my mother tell it, Nora was a 'brazen
hussy'.

My bitter Mom's one and only review of Irish literature.
She believed, as did many of her generation, that Joyce was
'a writer of pure filth'.

I moved quickly along that street, memories of my

mother not being my favourite ones, and into Cross Street. I like that one, it has the office of the *Connacht Tribune*, and you want local news, that's the paper you need. There's a nice vibe here, and just along, parallel to Shop Street, is the situation for the Saturday market. But gee, guess what, they were talking about demolishing it and getting rid of the market. Galwegians would die before they let the fucks get away with this.

I hope.

I hit St Nicholas' Church, where they say Columbus prayed before setting off to find America.

Must have been some powerful plea.

And here I was in Shop Street, three minutes from the pub.

A guy stopped, said, 'Jack?'

I stared at him. Nope, didn't know him, but what had that to do with anything? Since the shooting, it seemed everybody knew me.

He was dressed from head to toe like an advert for American sport. A sweatshirt for the LA Dodgers, track pants with a stripe down the leg and a logo that read SUPERBOWL, plus the requisite Nike trainers. Perched precariously on his head was a baseball cap that read KNICKS KICK ASS. I have to say I was dazzled by the sheer amount of Americana. He wasn't young, so no excuse there, he was in his mid sixties, or else very badly blasted from drink or drugs or both.

He said, 'I was a friend of your mother's.'

Which meant he was no friend of mine. He registered my response and added, 'I mean your late lamented mother.'

He blessed himself, said, 'May the Lord give her peace. He certainly didn't give her much while she walked the earth.'

I was going to say that she didn't provide a whole lot of that commodity herself, but what was the point? He'd reckon I was bitter, which was true.

I asked, 'You stopped me for?'

He gave a well-rehearsed laugh – someone must have told him it was one of his best features. They lied.

I looked at my watch and he took the hint, said, 'Here I am delaying you. The thing is, I'm collecting for the under-fourteen football team, we want to get them some new gear.'

I stared at his outfit and asked, 'Will it bear any relation to what you're wearing?'

He was horrified. 'They play Gaelic. I mean, we have to support our national game.'

Before he could launch into some long-winded lecture on the history of hurling, I said, 'Tell you what, I'll put a cheque in the post, how would that be?'

Not good.

I was waving goodbye before he could formulate a reply.

Just before I got to Garavan's, someone else hailed me and I went *Fuck off*. There is only so much shite you can take in one morning and I was way past my quota. I got inside quickly. The barman nodded, no words, which was fine and I went into the snug. You are finally part of the furniture when not only do you not order anything but head for your own seat and wait for the drinks to arrive.

As they did.

The pint looked like all the prayers I'd ever hoped to have answered. The Jameson, riding point, was its own glory.

I muttered, 'Doesn't get any better than this.'

How sad is that?

As the barman put the drinks down, I wondered if I should ask him his name. But then we'd probably get friendly and something terrible would happen to him. So I simply grunted and he asked, 'Did you see the pilot of *Deadwood* on Sky last night?'

I'd been in bed by nine, having taken another sleeper to ease the pain that had erupted in my heart. I shook my head.

'It was mighty, real dirty, wild, the language was ferocious. I counted *fuck* thirty times.'

Is there an answer to this? An answer that falls on any level of sanity? I didn't have it.

He added, 'You'd love it.'

Now is that flattering or asking for a slap in the mouth? I let it slide, resolving to catch the next episode.

I was about to leave when a guy walked in, looked round, approached me, asked, 'Can I get you a whiskey?'

I've seen many men, women too, wrecked by booze, their faces a testament to all that hell has to offer, but this guy, he was like those photos of Bukowski in his last days. Not good. Beneath the ruin, I'd hazard he was only thirty or so, but the red eyes had seen things that a century of hurt might accomplish.

I asked, 'Is there a sign out there that says, *Gather here all ye nutcases – if you want to find a dog or just generally go bananas, then this is the shrine for you?*'

He fixed bloodshot eyes on me and repeated, 'Dog? What dog?'

I knew this could go on for a time so I cut to the chase, snapped, 'Were you looking for me?'

The question seemed to throw him and he disappeared. I wrote it off to the weather – storms bring out the crazies like a call to the wild. A tabloid was on the seat beside me and I glanced at the headlines, the lead story being BRITNEY'S SECOND WEDDING NOT LEGAL! This covered most of the front page, and in a corner was a small feature on the British hostage in Iraq. He'd been kidnapped with two Americans who had now been beheaded – his fate was literally hanging on a thread. His family had begged Tony Blair to help. Before I could turn to page three, where the story was continued, the guy was back, a large whiskey in his shaking fist.

He said, 'Sorry, man. I had to, like, get straight, get my act together.'

His body was in tremors. If this was him in shape, God forbid I'd ever witness him falling apart. I resolved to change pubs – it seemed the whole flaming town knew I was available in Garavan's. What disturbed me was he was so like me. The state of him, I'd been there so many times, and in my current guise was but a drink or two from his terrain.

He put out his hand. 'I'm Eoin Heaton.'

I took his hand. It was drenched in perspiration and after I withdrew mine I had to struggle not to wipe it. I felt the identification you have for a fellow sufferer but I didn't want to know, and was about to gently dismiss him when he said, 'I'm like you.'

Fuck.

As if he read my mind. I made to stand up. I really didn't need this shit and if he was seriously fucked, well, too bad, tough luck and all that, but hey, not my problem.

He said, 'I was a Guard and they threw me out.'

I sat back down, my own sad career flashing before me. He asked, 'Didn't you hit a politician, smack him right in the kisser?'

And had thus begun my glorious descent into years of pain.

His face had lit up at the thought of my action, the first sign of vitality he'd shown. I could see he was at heart a decent character, tinged with naivety but with an essential – what's the word? – goodness, if there's such a thing any more in a world where a pop star's mad marriages garner more newsprint than the imminent beheading of a man.

I said, 'Well, I have some regrets about that.'

He was eager to agree with me, asked, 'You're sorry you hit him?'

'No, I'm sorry I only hit him once.'

He gave a loud laugh, tinged with hysteria, then stopped abruptly, stared at me, asked, 'What's wrong with your voice?'

I was conscious that it was more guttural than usual, like I'd sucked in granite, and it had been paining me a lot in recent days.

I said, 'You smoke a thousand cigarettes and drink enough rotgut whiskey, it plays hell with your diction.'

He was torn between feeling bad for mentioning it and a certain excitement at being so close to someone who'd been . . . *at a shooting*. His curiosity won out and he asked, 'What was it like, if you don't mind me asking, you know, to . . . have that happen to you?'

What do you answer? That it was fun, and is the reason why you're smelling of raw whiskey at noon or that you're suffering, as the doctors warned, post-traumatic stress syndrome?

I opted for keeping it light. 'It ruined me whole day.'

He was nodding, as if he could imagine.

He couldn't.

I didn't have any more to add so I asked, 'What is it you want from me?'

Got a nervous smile. He looked at his now empty glass, as if to say, *How'd that happen?*

I knew the feeling.

He said, 'Lemme get us some fresh drinks.'

I wanted to, and having a bone fide drunk to keep me company, it should have been ideal, but I had parameters to keep.

'No, not for me, I've got to go.'

He was disappointed. Not quite the response he'd been expecting. He said, 'Can you help me?'

I liked him, but not that much.

I said, 'Get yourself into rehab, call AA, there's all –'

He cut me off, horror on his face, near shouted, 'Not that kind of help, Jaysus. A few days in bed, some paracetamol, bit of grub, some kickback time, I'll be fine.'

I thought, *Dream on, sucker* and waited.

He sat up straight, said, 'I want to do what you do. You know, find stuff, work on cases.'

I could have given him the lecture, told him he was buying a bucket of grief, but as I got ready to launch, he pleaded, 'Jack, I need a lifeline. I got nothing, I'm dying here. If you give me something to hang on to, I'll get back in shape. I just need, like, a focus.'

And yet again I made the wrong decision. Should have just set him adrift but he got to me, the expression in his eyes, that lost desperate cry.

I said, 'OK, I'm going to give you a start, and if you manage it, we'll see if maybe you can help me on some other stuff.'

He grabbed my hand, gratitude pouring out. 'You won't regret it.'

I was regretting it already, cautioned, 'You haven't heard what it is yet. You might not be so grateful in a moment.'

His face expressed the belief that wonderful events were about to occur. It's a result of Jameson on an empty stomach, the illusion that all will be well. I told him about the disappearance of the Newcastle dogs and my being asked to check it. I took out my notebook, gave him the name of the man who'd asked for my help. He looked really sick, not just drink sick but the illness that rides with acute disappointment. Took him a moment to digest the information and then he near spat, 'Fucking dogs – you want me to search for a missing frigging animal?'

I shook my head. 'I don't want you to do a blessed thing, I already told you that, but you said you were prepared to do anything. Here's your chance to prove it.'

He was wringing his hands, a gesture I thought was purely confined to books, and said, 'OK, I'll give it a shot.'

He was so far gone that the awful irony of his words escaped him.

There was resignation in his voice, the troubles of the world in his eyes, so I countered, 'Hey, listen up, you're not doing me any fucking favours. You have something else going on, then go for it, don't let me keep you from better things.'

He was wiped, looked at me with the face of a five-year-old boy, said, 'I'm sorry, Jack, I . . . I'll get right on it.'

I gave him my phone numbers and when he continued to sit there I said, 'Well, get to it. You think the solution's going to pop its head round the corner?'

As he reached the door he said, 'I understand now what they meant.'

To be rid of him I asked, 'Yeah, what was that?'

'That you're a hard bollix.'

He was gone before I could reply.

The barman came in, began to collect the glasses, asked, 'Get you anything else?'

'No, I'm good. You know that guy who just left?'

He wiped the table down, said, 'Heaton? You'd need to be careful of him.'

'Because he's a drinker?'

He gave a short laugh and glanced at me as if he wondered was I kidding, the kettle calling the pot black. He said, 'Well, there's that, but I meant he used to be a Guard. Them fuckers never change their spots.'

9

A drunk kneeling before the cross,
dying of a hangover, says to God,
'Come down, lemme up there for a while.'

After the funeral of John Willis, his family shut down. At home were his parents and his sister, Maria. For a few days, neighbours called, bringing food, condolences and very little actually to say. The manner of his death, crucifixion, brought all comments to a halt. What was to offer in the comfort line?

'He's better off.'

'Time eases all pain.'

'Only a hundred shopping days to Christmas.'

It was easier not to call, so the house gradually became filled with silence. Maria was inconsolable. She felt especially bad as she'd always been closer to their older brother, Rory, who was in England. She was nineteen, and had her first car, a secondhand Datsun with a lot of mileage on the clock. Maria was a plain girl, and all the make-up in the world only seemed to scream, *Christ, she's plain.* But when she got behind the wheel, she felt like a player, like she was important. Even, sometimes, that she might be pretty. She worked for a local building firm and they'd told her to take as much time off as she wished. A

Monday morning, she'd driven to Salthill, parked on the promenade and watched the ocean. She liked it when it was rough, the fierceness of the sea worked like a balm on her agonized heart. If she'd looked in the mirror, she'd have seen a girl sitting on a bench, a girl with dark hair and madness in her eyes. The girl was watching Maria with a ferocious intensity. From time to time the girl muttered, 'You're going to burn, bitch.'

My phone rang and I answered to my solicitor. He said a local auctioneer had asked if I'd consider selling my apartment. My initial reaction was no way, but for the hell of it I asked how much he was offering, and was near floored to hear the amount.

I went, 'For an apartment?'

I couldn't believe it.

He said, 'City-centre residences are like gold dust, and as an investment you can't lose.'

All my befuddled life I've made decisions on the spur of the moment, usually bad ones. Now I went, 'OK, let's do it.'

He was as surprised as I was, asked, 'You sure?'

'Of course not, but sell it anyway.'

I had long been thinking of making a major change to my life. If I continued as I was, Galway would kill me – it had very nearly done so already. Just like that, I decided to go to America. I'd said for years I'd love to go – now I could do it in some style, head down to Florida, find me a rich widow, lie in the sun.

Florida was in the grip of its fourth hurricane and I was

planning to go there. Par for the course of my life. First I'd hit New York, soak up the city, then mosey on down to Vegas and then south. I might even go to Mexico. My heart was pounding, my palms covered in perspiration and I realized I was excited at the thought of a new life. God, how long had it been since I'd been worked up about anything? I'd look into the crucifixion deal for Ridge, see if I could solve it and then take off, leaving all that shite behind me.

I got out the phone directory, rang a travel agent, booked a provisional departure to New York from Shannon. Put the phone down and thought, 'You're really going to do this.'

I was.

Who would I say goodbye to? Most all I knew were in the cemetery. I checked my watch. I wanted a drink to celebrate but stuck to my mad sensory deal. My head was a whirlwind of thoughts. They call it a racing mind, well, mine was accelerating at the speed of light. Thoughts of flight, like a shot of Crystal Meth, had galvanized my whole fragile nervous system. Mexico, I'd have to rethink that, as I had only just read Kem Nunn's novel *Tijuana Straits*. He wrote that really bad shit happened down there and I wondered, would this be different from my current life?

I would certainly be travelling light. What I owned could be put in an envelope and posted.

First, I had to talk to the dead boy's parents – I didn't want to, but if I was going to do this, then I had to visit. I'd have my coffee, strong, black and bitter, then head down and, if nothing else, extend my sympathies. I was sure that would make their day. Just what they needed, a total stranger saying how sorry he was and then asking them questions. Oh fuck, if only I was drinking – couple of drinks, I'd talk the hind leg off a donkey.

Do the maths:

> Disturbing a family in mourning = two large Jamesons.
>
> Being a nosey bollix = many, many pints of the black.
>
> New life on the horizon = one bottle of something fast and lethal.

Made mad sense to me, but then my excuse is I'm Irish and logic plays no part in my reasoning.

My feelings were mixed as I headed for the Claddagh.

The Claddagh is known worldwide because of the Irish wedding band: two hearts united and topped with a crown. In the centre is a heart. You wear the heart pointing out, you're looking for a partner; you wear it turned in, you're spoken for.

The Claddagh is a unique piece of history, not only of Galway but indeed of Ireland. Here you had a community of people living in almost an isolated village, nigh separate from Galway, even though the town was but a spit away. The main livelihood was fishing. Their boats were special, weighing anything from eight to fourteen tons. The men sailed all along the coast, and on their return their women, who made the nets, then sold the produce. Unlike other fishing boats of the country, the singular feature of these was the open deck. They were known as 'Hookers'.

Never ceases to amuse Americans.

And more's the tragedy, this self-sufficient community ceased to exist in 1934 when their homes were demolished to provide so-called more sanitary dwellings. They didn't use the term 'progress' then, but it was the same spirit of change and obliteration as was running riot today.

But the spirit, the sheer will of people from Claddagh, still exists, handed down through all these years, and even in a cosmopolitan city, Claddagh folk are their own distinctive breed.

Me, I love the place.

Used to be a time when feeding the swans was a real lift and not just for them. It was part of the Galway deal. And you'd look up, see Nimmo's Pier, and the ocean beckoning to you, calling you to a life that seemed ablaze with promise. On the horizon, the Aran Islands and a way of living that didn't entail hurry. But this was no longer a comfort zone for me. Too many scenes of violence and loss were tied up with the area.

I walked quickly through. A guy sitting at the water's edge was alternately feeding the swans and a greyhound. The dog was in bad shape, skinnier than a tinker.

I said, 'How you doing?'

Without looking at me he asked, 'Want to buy a greyhound?'

'Er, not right now.'

He shrugged as if it was my loss, added, 'This animal is a winner.'

Yeah.

I didn't want to delay, but some nonsense just has to be addressed, else you begin to believe that chaos really does rule. I asked, 'Why don't you race him your own self?'

He gave a laugh clogged with bitterness and regret, said, 'My missus, she hates dogs.'

Maybe she was the one stealing the Newcastle ones. He added, 'But I hate her, so it like, evens out, you know?'

On impulse I asked, 'Offhand, would you know why a person would snatch dogs from various houses?'

I thought he hadn't heard me or couldn't be bothered to answer so I moved on, but then he shouted, 'To eat them.'

Dare I say, food for thought?

I stood before the house, taking a moment to compose myself. The building was one of a terrace, small, rundown, with an air of poverty. I recognized it, as I'd grown up in one just like it. The small garden was well tended, some rose bushes defiantly facing the worst the North Atlantic had to throw. I popped a mint in my mouth. If you want the world to know you've been drinking, take one. It's like, *Hello, I'm disguising the smell of booze.* Even though I hadn't drunk, old habits die slow. Ask Sinn Fein.

I knocked once, then for good measure took another mint.

A man in his late sixties answered. He was small, with white hair and an air of defeat, black rings under his eyes.

'Mr Willis?'

He stared at me. 'Yes.'

I was about to launch in when he said, 'I know you.'

I waited, wondering if he was going to slam the door,

but he gave a small smile, his mouth contracting, like it had forgotten how to.

'You're the man who saved the swans.'

And then before I could respond, he said, 'Please come in.'

He ushered me into a dark hall, then shut the door quietly. 'In here, please.'

A spotless living room, with a flamenco dancer poised on top of the television, testament to happier times, perhaps. A cabinet with a glass front held trophies, photos and a line of *Reader's Digest*s.

He motioned for me to take a seat and said, 'I'll just get my wife. Would you like coffee, tea, or maybe something stronger?'

I declined, if not easily. I noticed a silver photo frame, the centrepiece on the cabinet, and moved closer. It showed three people: two young men and a girl. The dead man I recognized and the girl would be the sister, Maria, but the third? A line of T.S. Eliot ran in my head . . . something about a third who walks beside you. His hair was red but his resemblance to the other two was marked, he had to be a brother. I muttered, 'There is another brother?'

How had Ridge missed him? I'd need to check him out.

The silence in the house was unsettling. The father returned with a woman who looked even more defeated than him. Her body had folded in on itself.

She put out her hand and said, 'Pleased to meet you.'

Jesus.

I muttered some cliché about their loss and she nodded. I caught a glimpse of her eyes and wished to Christ I hadn't.

If there is a step beyond anguish, beyond torment, she was there. We stood, an awkward trio, no one sure what to do.

So I tried, 'I hate to intrude, but I'm looking into the circumstances of John's . . .' And for the life of me I couldn't find an apt word – death, demise, murder, all too harsh.

Instead of asking me on what authority I was thus engaged, she said, 'We're very grateful.'

Out of desperation, I asked if I could see his room and the father led me to a small back room. He said, 'We haven't touched anything.'

A young man's room: the bed unmade, a bookcase with car magazines, a CD player and a rack of music. I stood there and wondered what the hell I was doing.

After five minutes, I went back to the couple and asked, 'What was John like?'

Got an outpouring of love and affection. He was an ordinary lad – played football, worked in a garage, had lots of friends.

The front door opened and a girl came in. I knew instantly she was their daughter, from the photo on the cabinet. Hard to fool a professional investigator.

The mother said, 'We'll leave you with Maria. She and John were very close.'

After they'd shuffled out, she stared at me and asked, 'How is this any of your business? Did you know John?'

I said I didn't, but that as the Guards weren't making any progress, I wanted to see if maybe I could help.

She digested that, asked, 'Are you being paid?'

'No, but . . .'

She wasn't angry, just confused.

'So you're just a good guy who goes round helping out, righting wrongs, that it?'

Before I could answer, she said, 'You're full of shit.'

I felt on firmer ground. Aggression suits me best, none of that polite tiptoeing, so I said, 'I'd have thought you'd welcome any help available.'

She studied me for a minute, not much liking what she saw, then said, 'Who gives a fuck what you thought? John isn't coming back. Would you do me a favour?'

'Sure, if I can.'

'Leave us the hell alone. Would you do that? Go play Superman with someone who gives a fuck.'

Then she walked me to the door, her body language saying, You're gone.

As she watched me begin to walk away she said, 'Another thing, Mr Taylor, the mints don't work.'

I knew that, right?

Back at my apartment, I put on Tom Russell's *Road to Bayamon*. There's a bitter-sweet song there, 'William Faulkner In Hollywood'. Made me yearn for a better life and I had to stop it mid track. Rang Ridge. She sounded her usual hostile self.

'What?' she grunted.

'Did you know a Guard, Eoin Heaton?'

A pause as she weighed up the reason I might be inquiring.

'Yes, I knew him. Why?' Her voice was dripping with aggression.

'They kicked him out, right?'

A sigh and then, 'Yes, he suffered from your complaint.'

I didn't need to ask what that was, so I tried 'Was he any good, as a Guard?'

She waited a beat, then said, 'They threw him out. How good could he have been?'

I wanted to shout at her, tell her to climb down off the bloody high horse, but instead asked – and I had to strain, no doubt about it, I was literally finding it hard to hear – 'What did he do, apart from drink? What were the grounds for dismissal, or are you sworn to secrecy?'

'He took a bribe to let a man off a drink-driving charge.'

I hadn't anything to say so she added, 'You probably approve of that, and think he was harshly dealt with.'

Enough, I thought, so I lashed out with, 'How would you know what I think?' Then I took a deep breath and asked, 'Did you know John had a brother? I've been to see the family, met the parents and the sister. I really think – and it's a strong feeling, a gut instinct – that you should find out about this brother. Can you do that? Anything, everything on him you can get.'

She was silent for a moment, then asked, 'You really think it's that important?'

'Absolutely.'

I at least had her attention and just before she hung up she said, 'OK, what's to lose?'

After I'd put the phone down, I was actually feeling pleased with my own self and realized that for once I was driving this whole gig onwards.

10

'I think you've forgotten me.'

Hostage Ken Bigley in a message to Tony Blair,
twenty-four hours before he was beheaded.

I'd been bothered for some time by a problem I was trying to ignore, felt if I didn't acknowledge it, it would just go away.

Yeah.

My hearing.

With the television, I had to turn it to max volume, and my music, top level too. And when people spoke to me, I had to lean in close to catch what they said. You hit fifty, things are going to start to decay. Fact of frigging life. My eyes were still OK, but the life I'd led, it was a miracle I was still above ground. Lots of days, I wished I wasn't.

So I got out the telephone directory, found an ear specialist and made an appointment, straining to hear what the receptionist said. Jesus, if I lost me hearing . . . I already had a limp . . . how old was that?

No point in sharing with Ridge, she said I never listened anyway. I admitted to me own self – a thing I hated to do – I was scared. I was alone. Your Irish bachelor in all his pitiful glory, shabby and bitter, ruined and crumbling.

With a plan.

Christ Almighty, a plan. Me whole physical being was shutting down and I had a plan. Isn't that priceless? Here I was, on me last legs, and instead of planning for a retirement home, I was heading for America. Can you beat that?

You could say I was fighting back, showing fortitude in the face of fierce adversity, refusing to lie down, fighting the good fight. And anyone who knew me would savour this fine line of reasoning then utter, 'Bollocks.'

A morning shrouded in despair. In Irish we moan, *Och ocon* . . . Woe is me, with bloody knobs on. I'd been in deep depression for nigh on two weeks. No drinking, of course, not because I didn't want to or think it a good idea, but I didn't think I'd another round of so-called recovery in me.

Watched telly in betwixt times. The news was ferocious in its darkness.

Ken Bigley was beheaded. There are no words to describe how that felt, like seeing the Twin Towers get hit. The same disbelief, the same sick horror. I went into a further spiral of black dog and dreamed of dogs – yes, the Newcastle ones. They howled and bit at my ankles, barking for me to *do something*. The phone rang continuously. I jerked the plug out of the socket and I swear it still rang.

Odd times, people pounded at my door and I mumbled, 'Fuck off, I gave at the office.'

In such delusions, you always get to hear the phantom orchestra, like Malcolm Lowry described. Mine had one tune, over and over . . . 'Run', by Snow Patrol. I prayed that if I died – and it seemed highly likely – I wanted someone to play that at my funeral.

What a fucking song.

What a fucking life.

But if there was no one left to attend my passing, who was there to mourn me? Self-pity, of course, is the outrider of the DTs – and I was drenched in it. The country, too, was feeling pretty bad. We had rejoiced in our first Olympic gold medal for over thirty years, and sure, we made a huge deal of it. Who wouldn't? And then – you couldn't make this up – the horse failed the dope test. The frigging horse!

In a country where madness was respected and lunacy was a given, this was a step beyond.

When I finally got the strength to go out, shaky and paranoid, I met a woman who said, 'You know today is the blessing of the dogs?'

I stared at her and gasped, 'What?'

She seemed to think I should know and patiently explained, 'In the Poor Clare Convent, there's a special ceremony to bless the dogs.'

There are a hundred replies to this, all involving sarcasm and very weak puns, but all I said was 'Oh.'

I wondered if the dogs of Newcastle might be safer now. Somehow I doubted it.

I went to Garavan's, and before the barman could pour my usual I said, 'Black coffee and sparkling water. Galway Irish water, if you got it.'

My father would have turned in his grave to know the day had come when we paid for water on an island surrounded by the bloody stuff and lashed by rain most days of the year.

If the barman had any comment on my long absence, he kept it to himself.

It was the day of my appointment with the ear guy, and I'd dressed for bad news.

How do you do that?

Dress down, dress black.

I wore me funeral suit, bought from the charity shop. It had a sheen from overuse.

The Crescent in Galway is our answer to Harley Street. Translate as cash – lots of. Old listed houses, covered in ivy and decay, with nameplates on the front. No titles like Doctor, it was all Mister, denoting a consultant and mainly denoting it was going to be expensive. As they said in town, 'That's the Mister you'll well fucking earn.'

These old crumbling houses are the last barrier in a town with modern construction run riot. The developers circled these properties, waiting for an opportunity – a death in the family, bankruptcy – any window to move, offer shit-piles of cash and get the place in their portfolio. Then they'll rip the guts out of it or raze it to the ground, and presto, a new set of luxurious apartments, uglier with each successive purchase.

I liked these buildings as they stood: draughty halls, high ceilings, mildew in the corners, rising damp creeping along the walls, highly suspect floors, and the plumbing – don't even think about that. If you wanted to replace that, you'd need to win the Lotto. And cold – they were always freezing. It's a bizarre fact that the wealthy, the

Anglo-Irish, all have houses that would freeze your nuts off. Accounts for why they are always dressed in Barbours and thick woollen scarves, and of course why they're always out fox-hunting.

The Mister I had my appointment with was Mr Keating. He was dressed in a tweed suit – no white coats for these boyos – and he treated me with mild disdain, bordering on sarcasm. He did a whole range of tests, and I swear, like the doctor who'd examined Cody, he did that tut-tutting sound I thought was confined to the novels of P. G. Wodehouse.

Finally he was done. He put his hand on his chin and asked, 'Have you ever received a blow to the head?'

For a mad moment I thought he was threatening me, but then realized he was inquiring.

Me . . . a blow to the head. Count the ways, O Lord.

I said, 'I used to play hurling.'

He gave what might have been a smile but could have been wind. 'And no doubt, you being a macho type, you didn't wear a helmet?'

Fuck, we could barely afford to pay for the hurleys. Helmets? Yeah, sure.

He said, 'I may send you for an MRI, but I'm pretty sure my initial findings are correct.' He paused and I wondered if I would have to guess. Then he continued, 'Your left ear, due to an injury, or perhaps simply age, is showing signs of degeneration – very rapid degeneration – and within a short time you will be completely deaf in that organ.'

Degeneration.

What a fucking awful word.

He began to scribble on a pad.

'Here is the name of a very fine hearing-aid man. He'll fit you with one.'

I was trying to play catch-up. 'I have to wear a hearing aid?'

Now he smiled.

'Enormous advances have been made in this field. You'd barely notice the newest models.'

Easy for him to say.

And that was it.

He said, 'My secretary will provide billing.'

Naturally. That I heard without any trouble.

I was at the door when he added, 'If you feel compelled to continue hurling, do use a helmet.'

I couldn't resist, said, 'Bit late, wouldn't you say?'

I met with Eoin Heaton. He was if anything even more bedraggled than before, and the booze was leaking out of his very skin. A stale, desperate smell.

He opened with, 'I've been on this dog thing, like, day and night.'

Sure.

I stared at him. It was like looking in a mirror, all the days I'd racked up in a similar condition. We were in a coffee shop in a side street near the Abbey church. The owner of the place was a Russian who had bought it from a Basque. You have to wonder, where did all the Irish go? We may have got rich but we sure were outnumbered. The latest figures showed that by 2010 Ireland would have one million non-nationals.

Heaton had a black coffee and I opted for a latte, which is frothy milk disguised as caffeine.

Heaton tried to bring the cup to his lips, but his hands shook too much. He said, 'I should have had a straightener.'

Meaning a cure, the hair of the dog and all the other euphemisms that disguise the lethal jolt of alcoholism in full riot.

He reached in his pocket, asked, 'Would you mind, Jack?' and slipped a small bottle of Paddy across to me.

The small bottle, holding my own death warrant, looked so innocent. I unscrewed the top, glanced over at the owner, who was preoccupied, and then poured the booze into his cup. Paddy is one of the strongest whiskeys and the scent was overpowering. I held the cup to his lips and he managed to get half of it down, then did the dead man's dance of choke, gulp, gargle, grimace. He finally managed to utter, 'I think . . . think it might stay down.'

It did, barely.

Then the sea change, within minutes.

Like a demonic miracle, all darkness, it did not come from any place of light. His eyes stopped watering, a rosy colour spread across his face and his hands ceased their jig. He changed physically, his posture became erect and a note of defiance hit his mouth. But I knew – Jesus, did I ever – how short-lived it would be.

I heard him ask – no, demand – 'You deaf or something?'

Right.

I asked, 'What?'

He sighed. 'I've spoken to you twice and you didn't answer.'

If I turned my right ear towards him I could hear better, so I did and said, 'Run it by me one more time.'

With exaggerated slowness he said, 'The case you assigned me? Two more dogs were taken in Newcastle.'

Sarcasm dripped from his lips.

He wanted to fuck with me, he'd picked the right time.

I snapped, 'So what are you doing about it? Christ, you used to be a Guard, you can't find a dog-stealer?'

He reeled from the lash. Paddy has only so much power.

He stammered, 'It . . . it . . . takes time to get my shit together.'

I wasn't letting up, said, 'If it's too much for you, I can get someone else, someone who doesn't reek of stale booze.'

I'd hurt him and I wasn't sorry, not one bloody bit.

He tried, 'I'm on it, Jack. Honest to God, I can handle it, I won't let you down.'

I threw some notes on the table and as he eyed them I said, 'It's for the coffee.'

His eyes had the look of a broken child and he asked, 'Could you maybe advance me some cash?'

Without skipping a beat I replied, 'So you can piss it up against a wall? Get me some results and we'll see then.'

As I turned to leave he said, 'You're one hard bastard.'

I smiled. 'This is me on a good day, mate.'

And then the silence . . . Out of nowhere, I was enveloped in this eerie quiet, as if everything had stopped. I thought at first it might be as a result of my ear examination, some late kick-in, an aftershock, if you will. But no, it was an utter stillness, the kind that survivors describe when they attempt to articulate the moments before a disaster. I literally couldn't hear a thing. I was walking but couldn't hear my feet on the footpath. I was alarmed but not yet panicked. And then . . .

Then my phone shrilled.

I pulled the phone out of my pocket, realized my heart was pounding, pressed the little green key.

'Mr Taylor?'

'Yeah?'

'This is the hospital. You'd better get up here.'

'What, is it Cody? Is he all right?'

'Please get here as soon as you can, Mr Taylor.'

Hung up.

I don't much believe in anything no more, but attempted, 'Oh God, let him be OK. I'll be better.'

Whatever 'better' meant, I'd no idea.

11

. . . And burn in Hell.

Maria Willis just could not get past the death of her brother. That he had been crucified only added to the horror in her head. John had been a gentle soul. In a world of chaos, cruelty and sheer indifference, he'd been almost childlike. Her impulse had always been to mind him. She couldn't help wondering if he'd thought of her as they drove the nails into his hands.

The only comfort she could find was to drive out to Salthill, sit and watch the ocean. It calmed her, she didn't know why, it simply eased the agony she carried in her heart.

Thursday evening, she was sitting again, parked down from the old ballroom. Her parents had danced to the show bands there. Before the tragedies, her father would recite the names of the bands like a rosary, the names slipping from his mouth with obvious delight: the Clipper Carlton, the Regal, the Miami, Brendan Bowyer with his famous dance, the Hucklebuck. Once, he and her mother had demonstrated this particular oddity. It consisted of sliding both feet and moving like you had a greyhound on your arse. They had all fallen about laughing and her mother had said, with deep warmth, 'You might laugh, but that dance was the craze of the country.'

Maria would have given her soul to be back in the kitchen, watching her parents, sweat pouring off them, delight on their faces, and her brothers smiling, despite their efforts to appear unmoved.

A tap on the window of her car. She looked to see a wild-haired girl, her eyes heavy with mascara and dressed all in black, a young man behind her. The girl was one of those – what did they call them? – Goths?

She rolled down the window, wondering if they were going to ask for money. The girl said with an English accent, 'So sorry to bother you, but we have information about your brother.'

Maria was taken by surprise and when the girl moved to open the door, Maria let her. The girl sat in the shotgun seat, and the man – more boy, really – got in the back. Maria didn't like him behind her.

The girl smiled reassuringly and said, 'It must have been very hard for you, the awful way that John died. He must have suffered so.'

Maria thought she detected a sneer in the words and the girl's eyes, they were definitely . . . malevolent. She began to regret her rashness in allowing them into the car.

The girl said, 'Grief, it just kills you, don't you think?'

Maria looked through the windscreen, but no one was about. The evening was cold and the usual walkers had stayed at home.

She asked, 'You said you had information about . . . John?' It hurt even to utter his name.

The girl was fumbling in her bag. She produced a lighter and asked, 'You smoke?'

And the boy grabbed her from behind, holding her tight in a vice-like grip.

The girl produced a small can of petrol and began to douse Maria, saying, 'Juice you right up, girl.' Then she flicked the lighter, opened the door of the car, said, a smile on her lips, 'You're cooking now,' and set the flame on Maria's jacket. A whoosh followed instantly and Maria could have sworn she heard the boy say, 'I'm so sorry.'

They were halfway down the prom when the flames hit the tank. The explosion sounded unbearably loud.

The girl did a little ballet step and let out a holler:

'Way to go, girl.'

12

How the flame ignites . . .

The girl's eyes opened. She'd been dozing and now snapped awake. She took in her surroundings, this awful room in such stark contrast to the home her mother had kept. And dampness, the whole house reeked of it. Blame the Irish weather? No, just a cheap landlord.

A slight smile curled on her lips as she thought, 'Can introduce him to the flame too.'

Even as she thought it she could smell smoke, a burning not too far away, and she allowed the scent to engulf her, to lift her up.

She was delighted, and emitted a series of giggles before wrapping her arms round her thin frame, hugging to herself the stark fact that she'd now killed twice. It gave her a rush of such adrenalin and power, it was like a whole new mode of intoxication. And yet she was still dissatisfied. More . . . she needed more.

Out of the corner of her eye she saw a whoosh of flame. It started in the corner of the room and crept along the wall, but when she turned to look at it directly, it vanished. When this occurred, as it did more and more, she usually checked people around her to see their response. She couldn't believe they hadn't seen it – but no, they seemed oblivious. This just confirmed that the darkness had chosen her. Only she could hear and act out the dark scenario, the malignant blueprint of revenge.

Her heart accelerated with images of fire.

She recalled the flight to Ireland with Aer Lingus, the cabin crew asking if they were going on holiday. There had been flames in the corner of the cabin – couldn't they see them? She'd smiled and said, 'Oh yes, a family outing. We're going to have us a high old time.' She'd waited before adding, 'Our mother is already over there.'

The crew had thought it was refreshing to meet such a close-knit family and had promised, 'You'll love Ireland.'

She'd pulled her eyes away from the inferno she could glimpse along the wings of the plane and replied, 'And Ireland is going to love us.'

13

There is no pain like the loss of a child.

I could have caught a cab to the hospital, but I wanted to delay the news that I dreaded I was going to hear.

Cody had come to me asking to be my partner in investigation, and he was a mix of naivety, pseudo-American swagger, irritation and aggravation.

Then the amazing thing had happened. I hate to go New Era but we . . . fuck it, we bonded. I began to love the kid. He was annoying as hell, but would suddenly do something that tore at my heart, like buy me a very expensive leather jacket. I was wearing it when he was shot, his blood all over the front. I burned it.

We'd had one memorable day when we went to a hurling match, bought the team's scarf, shouted like banshees, had a huge slap-up meal after and near hugged at the end of a perfect day.

I was something then that I, oh, so rarely have ever been – I was happy.

But *mo croi briste* . . . me heart is broken.

Let me put it this way: those whom the Irish gods would

destroy, first they give a shard of joy to. Least it's how they fuck with me and often.

A few people had asked then if he was my son. I was delighted and was beginning to see him as such. A chance of family, the dream I'd never even allowed me own self to entertain.

When the sniper shot those holes in him, the shots burned a wound in my soul that would never close.

I'd been round and round with speculation as to who had done the shooting. The stalker I'd dealt with for Ridge had a solid alibi; Cathy Bellingham, wife of my best friend Jeff, sure had cause – I'd been responsible for the death of her three-year-old daughter – but she'd disappeared and I was in no hurry to find her. The third possibility was Kate Clare, sister of Michael who might have beheaded a Father Joyce and whom I'd pursued to the gates of hell. Among the more awful aspects of this was that I actually liked Michael Clare, and Christ, as a victim of clerical molestation he'd already suffered the torment of the damned before he killed himself. Kate, it transpired, had flown off to the Far East and her whereabouts were currently unknown.

Truth is, I didn't care who had done the shooting. All I wanted was for Cody to be returned to me and then I'd deal with the shooter, whoever the fuck it was. And deal biblically.

I got to the hospital, my heart in me mouth, went up to the ward and met a nurse. She knew me from my daily visits, even used my first name.

She went, 'Oh Jack, I'm so sorry.'

Dizziness hit me, but before I could even catch my breath, a couple approached and the nurse said, 'It's Cody's parents.'

They had the look. That horrendous expression of sheer disbelief.

The man, in his late sixties, wearing a good suit, his face a mask of rage, snarled, 'You're Taylor?'

I nodded, still reeling from the implication of the nurse's opening line.

He spat in my face.

'You got our son killed, you bastard.'

His wife pulled him away and as she dragged him down the corridor, he shouted, 'I hope you burn in hell.'

There was literally a beat of silence – one of those moments of pure quiet when a terrible curse has been laid on a human being. All present froze in a tableau of pure shock.

My legs began to tremble. I don't mean a slight shake, I mean the full-on tremor that signals a major collapse.

The next hour or so is hazy. I think I asked if I might see Cody, but I'm not sure. For some bizarre reason, I found myself in the café downstairs, a cup of coffee before me and devastation all around me.

'Are you all right?'

I looked up to see a woman in her late forties, with a good solid face, long dark hair, huge eyes and – odd how the mind can work on some level – a slight accent. English was not her first tongue.

I almost accused, 'You're not Irish?'

119

She gave a small smile. 'You need someone Irish?'

What the fuck was this?

I said, 'I don't need anyone.'

For a moment, it seemed like she might touch my hand and that would have been a huge mistake. Instead, she said, 'You are in pain. Did you lose someone?'

My oldest ally, rage, was waiting to strike. I let the dog loose and snapped, 'Who the fuck are you? Leave me alone.'

She stood up, said, 'My name is Gina. I sense you are a good man and I can help you,' and pushed a business card towards me.

I said, 'Sense this – I want you to fuck off.'

She did.

I dunno why – madness, perhaps – I put the card in my jacket.

Then I was outside and it was raining heavily. I muttered, 'Good, hope I catch me death.'

Just outside the main door of the hospital, a veritable cloud of smoke near obscured the entrance. Not from the weather, no . . . the smokers, huddled like frightened lepers. The smoking ban was a year old now and these groups of social outcasts were a familiar sight, frozen in winter, laughing in summer – if you can ever call a summer in Ireland such.

A new term had been coined as nicotine romances had sprung up. People got talking; in their allied addiction, social barriers that might have taken much longer to over-come were now literally so much smoke. The flirting thus was termed Slirting . . . Flirting with the smoke.

I reached for me cigs and remembered I didn't smoke any more, didn't drink either. No, I was too busy killing all I cared for.

If one of the smokers had noticed my gesture and offered me one, I probably would have taken it. My eyes were locked on the River Inn, clearly visible from where I stood. I began to move.

I was at the hospital gate when I heard,

'Jack?'

And now fucking what?

A man in his early thirties, well dressed if casual, a good-looking guy but with a wary air about him. It was that that triggered my memory.

'Stewart?'

My former drug-dealer. He'd been busted, got six years and then hired me to investigate the supposed accidental death of his sister. That case had been among the worst I'd ever been involved with and led to the death of Serena May, the Down's Syndrome child of Jeff and Cathy.

He smiled, a smile of no warmth. I suppose if you do hard time in prison, warmth isn't going to be one of your characteristics. The time I'd gone to see him in jail, his front tooth had been knocked out and that was just what was visible. I noticed the tooth had been replaced. And his eyes – when I'd first met him, his eyes had been full of energy, and now they were pools of granite.

He asked, 'Are you OK? You look like someone died.'

How to answer that? Fall at his feet and bawl like a baby? Go hard ass and say, 'No biggie'?

I said, 'People are dying all the time.'

He considered that, then said, 'I have a new flat, just down the road. You want to come have a drink . . . ?'

He paused, added, 'Or a coffee?'

My drink history was known to all and sundry. I said, 'Why not?' and we began to walk towards St Joseph's Church. Before we got a chance to speak, a Guard's car passed, the cops giving us the cold scan.

Stewart watched them cruise slowly by and after they'd passed he said, 'They never let you move on.'

Amen.

His flat was near Cook's Corner. The pub there, almost a Galway landmark, had a FOR SALE sign, but then what hadn't?

Cook's Corner is literally the centre where three roads cross. You can walk down Henry Street, the canal murmuring to you on both sides, or turn and head north to Shantalla, literal translation being 'old ground' and still home to some of the best and most genuine people you could ever hope to meet. Or you could retrace my path, back to the hospital. There was a fourth option, but no one ever mentioned it; a fourth road that was there, but never alluded to: the route to Salthill. Years ago, it led to Taylor's Hill (no relation) and housed the upper classes. You had money or notions, you lived there. So it was never referred to by the people, money and notions not being on the agenda. But times, they were a-changing and Cook's pub was about to open the door to all sorts of speculators suddenly taking an interest in what had always been described as the poor man's part of town.

You think I'm kidding?

There were three charity shops on this patch alone.

We went into a plain two-storey house and he opened a door on the ground floor, said, 'Welcome to my humble abode.'

I never believed people actually used such clichés. What was next, *Mi casa es su casa*?

I have seen houses and apartments of all descriptions, and lots of them were bare, due to poverty or neglect or both. Shit, I grew up in one. We had a few sticks of furniture, and one particularly rough winter we used the kitchen chairs for the fire.

You think I'm talking about Ireland in the last century – would it were so. My father worked hard, but there were times the work just wasn't there. My mother would put his best and only suit in the pawn. That same pawn shop is now located in Quay Street, the trendiest area in our new rich shining society.

Stewart's place was the barest accommodation I've ever seen, and I've seen Thomas Merton's cell in photos. There was one chair, hard back, a tiny sofa, and two framed quotations on the wall.

Stewart was amused at my reaction.

'Bare, eh?'

I let out my breath, went, 'You moving in or out?'

He spread his hands in a futile gesture.

'Prison teaches you lots of stuff – sheer random cruelty, for one, and that's just the wardens; and more importantly, the bliss of nothing. I've been studying the Zen Masters, and with a bit of time I'll be still.'

I wanted to go smart arse, say, 'Still what?'

But said, 'The only Zen I know is pretty basic.'

He waited and so I muttered it:

'After the ecstasy

The laundry.'

He laughed, there was actually a little warmth in it.

'Trust you, Jack. That is so typical of what you'd choose.'

I could have argued the toss, but the truth was, I couldn't get past Cody. I could see him the first time he'd offered me the business cards, his whole face a light of eagerness and desire to please. A shudder hit me and my whole body began to shake.

Stewart went, 'Whoa there, big guy. Take a pew, I'll get you something.'

I sat on the hard chair, naturally – keep it rough – and Stewart reappeared with a glass of water and two pills.

'Take these.'

I held them in the palm of my hand and said, 'I would have thought you'd had enough of the dope business.'

The insult didn't faze him. He motioned for me to take the stuff and I did, washing it down with the water. He said, 'I'm out of the trade but I keep some . . . essentials here. I got out of prison, but that doesn't mean I'm ever free of it. I wake in the night, covered in sweat – I'm back there, some thick gobshite from the middle of the bog trying to stick his dick in my backside. I don't think I need to explain panic attacks to you, Jack.'

Carve that in Connemara stone, or better yet, Zen it.

His mobile rang and he said, 'Gotta take this. You just sit there, be still.'

What's the biblical line? Be still and know?

Know, as the Americans say, 'It sucks.'

I zoned out, went away to that place of white nothing-ness. The mind shuts down and there's a slight humming to be heard, and if you could see your own eyes, they'd have that nine-yard stare.

Then Stewart was back, I looked at my watch and nearly an hour had passed. I was mellow, laid back, tranquillized, thank fuck, feeling no pain.

I stood, moved to the wall, read one of his framed quotes. It went:

'The fundamental delusion of reality is to suppose that I am *here* and you are out there.'

The attribution was to some fellah named Yasutani.

I said, 'Deep.'

Stewart considered it, then said, 'At the risk of repeating myself, I think that describes you also.'

Whatever those pills were, they were the bloody business. I felt relaxed, a concept that was as alien to me as niceness, and my mind was clear. It wasn't till then that I realized how burdened it had been with fear, grief and worry about Cody. Can you be saturated with sorrow, seeped in sad-ness, a walking mess of melancholy?

I was.

I asked, 'You ever hear of Craig McDonald?'

He simply stared at me.

'He was a newspaper editor in Ohio and became a bestselling novelist. He wrote a novel about pain that would pull the teeth from your skull,' I said.

He thought about it, then said, 'Your kind of book.'

I sighed. 'Reading about it makes you feel you're not alone.'

He handed me a vial of pills. 'More of the same. You get the rush of panic, you drop some of those beauties and you'll, like, chill.'

He used the American expression with more than a hint of malice.

I said, 'You've been pretty damn helpful to me.'

He shrugged and I had to know, asked, 'Why?'

He was surprised, took a moment to gain composure then said, 'You proved my sister's death was not some drunken accident, so I owe you.'

I didn't want that. 'Hey, pal, you paid me, paid me well. Debt's cleared, done deal, you can move on.'

He smiled, a tinge of sadness in there, and said, 'You probably won't accept this, you being such a hard arse and all. The front you like to project – nothing gets to ol' Jack Taylor. Me, I see you different. I like you. Sure, you're a pain sometimes and God knows, you got a mouth on yah. But bottom line, you're that rarity, you're a decent human being. Flawed, oh fuck, more flawed than most, but you're not cold. And trust me on this, after my time in Mountjoy I'm a goddamn expert in the sheer coldness of the human condition.'

Some speech.

I made to go, said, 'You give me more credit than is warranted, but . . . thanks.'

He handed me a card.

126

'My phone numbers. You want to talk, get into some Zen, I'm around.'

I had to know. 'You still peddling dope?'

It hurt him and he winced a little. 'Like I said, you've a mouth on you, but am I dealing? Sure, but not dope.'

He wasn't offering any more so I shook his hand, which amused him, and I was out of there.

The drunk and the dealer, a match made in a moment of surreal tenderness. But what do I know? Tenderness is not my field.

I muttered aloud, 'Still . . . ?'

As Zen as it gets.

14

And upon this cross . . .

Next day, I got a call from the nurse I'd befriended at the hospital and she told me the details of the funeral and suggested, with apprehension in her tone, 'Mr Taylor, maybe it would be better if you don't attend.'

I was lost for a reply, felt like I'd been walloped in the face.

She rushed on, 'His parents, they . . . er . . . they are demanding that you be . . . kept away.'

I tried, 'I understand.'

I didn't.

She was a good person and they are as rare as common courtesy. I said, 'Thank you for being so helpful.'

Her last words were, 'We know you loved the boy. We see patients neglected all the time, but you came every day and you obviously didn't do it out of duty. God bless you, Mr Taylor.'

Fuck.

I'd have dealt better with outright antagonism, if she'd read me some warning act, threatened me not to go. Kindness only confused me. And she was wrong, I didn't visit Cody solely out of love. Pure guilt was there too and I hated every moment of it.

I was in my apartment, the bottle of Stewart's pills in my hand, when a knock came at the door. I put the pills on the table and answered.

Ridge.

She looked rough, as if she hadn't slept in days. She was in uniform. I hadn't often seen her in the Ban Gardai rig-out and she cut a poor figure of authority, like a little girl playing at cops. Her eyes were red-rimmed and she – could it be? – she reeked of booze.

Ridge?

I said, 'Come in.'

She did, walking like she was carrying the weight of the world. She sat down on the sofa, sank into it.

I asked, 'Get you something – a tea, coffee, glass of water?'

Took her a moment to answer and I thought she'd nodded off, then she said, 'I need a drink. What you got?'

The years she'd busted my balls about alcohol. The lectures and rants about my drinking, and now she wanted a drink *from me*?

I couldn't help it, snapped, 'You want a drink *from me*?'

She said sadly, 'Who would understand better?'

Ridge had said some rough stuff to me over the years, but this, this reached me in ways I didn't even want to analyse. I wasn't sure how to deal with a Ridge who was vulnerable.

She said, 'The death has thrown me.'

Now I was, to borrow her word, *thrown*. She didn't even know Cody.

I shouted, 'You didn't even know him.'

She sat up, turned to look at me, asked, 'Him? What are you talking about? It's not a him – it's the boy's sister, Maria.'

My blank look infuriated her and she nigh shouted, 'The crucified boy. You've forgotten him already, even though you promised to look into it. Well, don't bother. His sister, Maria, they burned her, in her car. Only her driving licence and teeth identified her. Everything else . . . everything else . . . was burned to a . . . fucking crisp.'

The room danced in front of me. I couldn't take in what she'd told me and I had to lean against the wall for balance.

She stood up, concerned now, asked, 'Jack? Jack, you all right?' And put out her hand.

I brushed it away, took some deep breaths and began to ease down a bit.

She backed off then asked, 'You said *him*. Who were you talking about?'

My throat was constricted, as if something was lodged there.

Finally I managed, 'Cody, he died. Yeah, the little bastard just packed it in, and guess what? – you'll love this – the family don't want me to attend the funeral. How do you like them apples?'

She slumped back in the sofa and said, 'You'll have to go and buy me some alcohol, you hear me.'

And why the fuck not?

The world had turned so nuts, it made a sort of Irish demented sense. I said in a cheerful party voice, 'Yeah, I will. You just relax your own self and I'll do what I'm best at, buy the hooch.'

The off-licence guy knew me, and as I loaded a basket with vodka, mixers, Jameson, he eyed me warily. I threw in peanuts and crisps and asked, 'How much?'

He knew I'd been dry for quite a time and seemed about to say something till I glared at him, daring him to go for it. I'd have dragged him over the counter. He rang up the stuff.

As I paid him I said, 'Isn't it wonderful I'm not smoking?'

He didn't answer.

The bollocks.

My mobile rang. I pulled it from my jacket. My ears were acting up – what wasn't? – but I heard, if badly,

'Jack, it's Eoin Heaton.'

He sounded drunk.

'The fuck do you want?'

He was stunned, I could hear it in his gasp, and he said, 'I found the dog-nappers.'

Jesus.

Dogs, now?

I said, 'And what, you want a medal? Try to remember you used to be a Guard. Use some initiative, solve the frigging thing.'

There was a note in his voice I should have caught. He said, 'But Jack—'

I didn't let him finish, said, 'And try not to be bribed, OK? Isn't that why they fucked you out of the force?'

*   *   *

I got back to the apartment and plonked the bag of booze on the table.

'I wasn't sure what to get, so I got everything.'

She waved her hand in vague dismissal, so I opened the vodka, poured a glass I'd have considered healthy, added some mixer and handed it to her. She grabbed it, downed half, let out a deep sigh. I swear, I could feel the stuff hit me own stomach. I went into the kitchen, made some coffee, got two of Stewart's pills and washed them down.

Bizarre aspect of addiction: even though you know the pills will help you, mellow you on down, you'd trade them in a second for the sheer blast, the instant rush of raw alcohol.

I went out to Ridge, sat in the chair opposite her, asked, 'When was the girl killed?'

She was staring at her glass, empty now, with that expression I'd had so often. *How'd that happen?*

She said in dead monotone, 'I've been on duty for forty-eight hours straight. I heard the medical guy say she'd been torched – that's the word he used, like American television.'

I didn't offer her another drink. I'd done my part. She wanted to get plastered, she could do it her own self.

I said, 'So it's obvious someone is targeting the family. There's no drug connection, no vendetta we've turned up.'

Then a thought hit me.

'Did you get anything on the other brother?'

She had her notebook out, the heavy job I'd carried all

those years I'd been on the force. It gave me a brief pang for the past. She was scribbling fast.

She said, 'Yes, his name is Rory. He's in London, but we haven't been able to contact him yet.'

I'd been leaning into her and she suddenly pulled back, asked, 'Why are you stuck in my face? You deaf or what?'

I decided this was not the time to share my latest cross with her.

She was up now. As she buttoned her tunic she said, 'I'm going to get right on this.'

I cautioned, 'Shouldn't you get some sleep? I mean, they see vodka on your breath, not good.'

She had that face of pure ferocity, said, 'Fuck them.'

I liked her a whole lot better.

I indicated the booze. 'What am I going to do with this?'

Her eyes were like coal. 'You'll think of some use.'

I liked her less.

15

'Cross me, and I'll kill you.'

Old Galway threat

The girl was fingering the small silver cross she wore round her neck. She knew neither her father nor brother understood the significance the cross had held for her and her mother.

Her mother had been a fervent Irish Catholic, and marrying an Englishman only intensified her passion. Over and over she'd told the girl, 'Christ died on the cross for our sins, and the world will try to crucify you if you allow it.'

Logic didn't play a large part in this. If you have the Irish faith, massive guilt and a personality disorder, you're ripe for symbols. Her mother had fixated on the crucifix, her home ablaze with writhing Christs of every shape and size. Only the girl truly knew where this obsession had originated. She'd never told before and she wasn't about to share now. They were men, they'd never understand.

The girl stood up. She'd been kneeling, praying, not to a Catholic God but to this new dark power that so energized her. She moved to the mirror, saw the silver cross shine around her neck, and from the corner of her eye saw the now familiar flame light up the corner of the room.

Whoosh.

When she turned to look directly at it, it was gone.

She smiled.

The cross was Celtic, given to her on her sixteenth birthday by her mother, who had said, 'Never forget the cross.'

Her mother's secret, the whole reason for the cross, came vividly into her mind. She could see it like a scene from a movie. She'd been twelve, always hanging out of her mother's arms, and one evening, home early from school, she'd found her mother sobbing in the kitchen, an empty bottle of sweet sherry on the sink. Her mother never drank and in that state she'd hugged her daughter, told her how before she'd met the girl's father she'd had an abortion, said it was like being crucified, the sheer agony of the procedure.

Then she'd added, 'I pay every day of my life for that sin.' And she'd grabbed her daughter's wrist harshly, hurting her, and warned, 'If anyone ever does real damage to you, there's only one way to atone. Do you know what it is?'

The girl, terrified, had shaken her head, tears running down her face. Her mother had said, in a voice of pure ice, 'You nail them to the cross, as Our Lord was, and drive the nails in with all the passion that Our Saviour decreed to us.'

Thursday evening, I killed a man.

Least I think I did.

Certainly gave it my best shot.

I'd gone to the pictures – sorry, I just can't say *movies*. *Sideways* had been getting tremendous reviews – Paul Giamatti had that hangdog expression I so identify with, a Woody Allen for the new despair. But all the wine drinking got to me. I was never a wine buff, I liked me booze fast and lethal. I was starting to taste Merlot in me mouth, and of course with my dodgy hearing, despite the Dolby digital stereo, I had difficulty catching all the dialogue. So I baled.

As I left, the ticket guy asked, 'Didn't like it, huh?'

He had one of those Irish faces that are boiled – red cheeks, lobster lips, pale skin, and still the American accent.

'I liked it too much.'

He gave me a look, the one that says, 'Old dude, already *safoid* (Irish for mental).' And said, like he'd been born in Kentucky, 'Whatever stirs your mojo.'

Fuck.

A light drizzle was coming now. Nothing major, just enough to remind you that you were in the land of *baiste* (rain). I was wearing item 8234, me old Garda coat. Like me own self, it had been burned, beaten and trampled on, and still hung in there. I turned up the collar and was debating getting a takeaway kebab. Thing is, with that you really need a six-pack.

A man fell into step beside me – tall guy, beer gut, odour of garlic and Guinness emanating from his pores. He said, 'You're Taylor.'

Had an edge, a tone of menace, and I knew this was going nowhere good. I had to strain to hear him, not that

I really wanted to know whatever shite this creep was peddling. His whole body language screamed trouble.

'So?'

He was leaning in on me, crowding with his body, and said, 'Baby-killer.'

Winded me. Any mention of Serena May and my whole body went into spasm.

Before I could respond, he said, 'And now you got some poor kid killed as well.'

Cody.

I stopped. There is a small alley near my flat in Merchant's Road, and I moved my body in its direction. I said, 'I don't know who you are and I don't want to know. I'm taking that shortcut home, and if you're real smart, you won't follow me.'

I hadn't even raised my voice, a real dangerous sign, means I'm heading for the zone, the cut-off place, where all rules are off. I'd been lured into alleyways by some of the most vicious bastards on the face of the planet, had me teeth removed with an iron bar in just such an area. The past few years, I'd been on the receiving end of the beatings, and whatever else, I was all through with lying on some spit-infested ground, some gobshite kicking me head in. The rage that had been smouldering since Cody's death, his parents' reaction to me, not drinking, not smoking, it moved up that deadly notch.

It's a white hot/cold burn. If that's not too Irish a description. It electrifies your whole psyche and focus . . . fuck, it wipes the slate of all else. The sheer rush of impending violence is like a double of Jameson you've been denying yourself and then you grab the glass, gulp and wait for the blast.

The dumb bollocks, he laughed, said, 'You're running, you cowardly prick. It's what you do, isn't it, you piece of garbage? I'm going to beat the living daylights out of you.'

Perfect.

The chat was done.

There's an old saying, *The law is practised in court-rooms, justice is dispensed in alleys.*

I turned into the alley and he ran to catch up, going, 'Hey.'

I bent low, swung with my left elbow and caught him in the kidneys, sucker punch, and as he gasped, I turned, kicked his right knee hard. Caught him on the descent with my fist, breaking his nose, heard the bone go. Then stood back, let him catch on this was just the prelude. I was only limbering up, all the rage was out to play and by Christ, I was looking forward to it.

He managed to mutter, 'You broke my nose. Why'd you do that?'

He had that long lank hair that something lives in, something vile. I grabbed a strand of it and slammed his head into the wall, heard a soft crunch.

'You seeing stars yet? Because you fucking will, and for a long time to come.'

His hand was up and he groaned, 'OK, enough, I'm done.'

Done?

I leaned in real close, echoed, '*Done?* You kidding?

We're not even started. That was just the trailer, the coming attraction.'

Then I beat him systematically with every foul and filthy trick I'd learned both as a Guard and on the streets, and when I finished I was sweating from every pore. Blood ran down my hands and my teeth hurt from how tightly clenched they'd been.

I stared at the huddled heap and began to walk off. And then, call it pure badness, I paused, walked back and gave him two kicks to the side of his head with my boot, and said, 'Now we're done.'

Back at my apartment, I tore off my coat. Normally, after such an episode, first order of business would be a large Jameson. I downed two of Stewart's pills, made some tea, laced with sugar for shock, and examined my hands. They were in bad shape. The left was mainly blood, torn skin. Water, ice cold, took care of that. The right was more serious. The fingers might be broken, I thought. They'd been broken before so I knew that song.

I tried to make a splint but couldn't get it together, and as I rooted around I found a card.

Gina De Santio

And phone numbers underneath.

What was it she said? If I needed help? Well, let's see if she was full of smoke.

I dialled the number with difficulty, waited then heard, 'Si?'

Decided to go for it.

'This is Jack Taylor. You gave me your card in the canteen of the hospital, said if I ever needed help?'

I could detect sleep in her tone – see, detection is my profession.

Took her a moment, then, 'Ah yes, Mr Taylor. I didn't expect you to call.'

I was going to reply, 'So why'd you give me the fucking card?'

But said, 'I need help, now.'

To my amazement, she said, 'I will come.'

Life – or people – just when you've lost all hope in the fuckers, they surprise you. The reason I was still getting up in the mornings, I suppose. I gave her my address and said, 'Bring some stuff, I have broken bones.' Thinking that would give her pause.

It did, but then she said, 'I will be there in twenty minutes.'

Go figure.

Stewart's pills had kicked in by the time she arrived. She looked radiant, and I felt something I hadn't felt in, oh, such a long time. A stirring.

Fuck.

She was wearing an old Trinity sweatshirt, worn jeans, trainers and a tan raincoat. Her hair was swept back and she looked wonderfully dishevelled.

'I really appreciate you coming, seeing as you don't really know me.'

She was surveying my flat as only a woman can. Not exactly critical, though there was that, but more a total scan of the whole set-up, not missing a thing. Her eyes lingered for a moment on my curtains and I knew she was thinking, *And when were they washed?*

Guys think, *Where's the booze?*

She was carrying a Gladstone bag, and it looked like it had seen active service.

She said, 'I might know you better than you think. I qualified as a doctor, but I work as a therapist mainly.'

That slight trace of an accent was very attractive, as if she had to carve out the right pronunciation.

I asked, 'Get you anything – tea, coffee? Oh, and I have Jameson and vodka.'

She gave me a look that asked, 'This is a social occasion?'

She said, 'Sit down and let's see what you've done to yourself.'

She was thorough. She washed and cleaned the wounds, made those *hmmm* sounds unique to the medical profession, then applied a splint to the fingers of my right hand.

'Those fingers have been broken before, but I'm fairly sure they're not broken now. However we'd need an X-ray to be certain, and I'm thinking you're not in any hurry to get that done?'

My hands dressed and wrapped in light gauze, she stood back.

'You'll live, but get to a hospital tomorrow.'

I was feeling very laid back, not hurting at all and able to appreciate her scent – the scent of a woman and something else I couldn't quite identify, but I liked it.

She looked at her watch, a very slim Rolex, and said, 'I'll have that drink now, vodka with tonic. I'm not working tomorrow so I can lie in.'

I wanted to lie with her. Blame Stewart's pills.

She asked if I was hurting much and the addict in me said, 'Lie big.'

I did.

She took some pills from her bag, rationed them out as doctors do, with that measured concentration lest they give you one more than you could need.

She said, 'These are very strong. Don't take alcohol with them.'

I tried not to grab them. I was building a nice little stash of defence. I got her the drink, asked, 'Why did you come? I mean, it's – what's the term – highly irregular?'

She sighed and then I recognized the scent. Patchouli oil, like the hippies used to peddle. Don't know why, but it gave me hope. Of what . . . I don't know, it had been so long since I had any. I just took it without analysis.

She stared into her glass. I knew there were no answers in there. The illusion of them, sure, but nothing that would give you the truth.

She said, 'I am from Napoli. We grew up poor. I married an Irish doctor, it's a long story, he is gone now and we had one daughter, Consuelo, the most beautiful girl. She died three years ago.'

She took a decent wallop of the vodka and continued.

'I got to join the most exclusive club in the world – the family of victims. No one wants to belong, we share the pain that never goes away and we can recognize each other, even without words. To outlive your child, this is the greatest torment the world can send. And when I saw you, saw the expression in your eyes, I knew you had joined.'

I wanted to say, 'Bollocks, peddle your therapy in some other neighbourhood.' Not even the pills could still the anger I felt.

I said, 'I sure do appreciate your help, but don't make any assumptions about me and loss.'

It sounded as fierce as I intended.

She gave a tiny smile and nodded her head. 'I understand rage.'

I wanted to shake her, scream, 'Do you? Do you fuck.'

She said in a quiet tone, 'It's one of the five stages of grief.'

I was on me feet. 'Me? I've narrowed it down to two – anger and drinking.'

She stood up, said, 'I must go. I would like to spend some time with you, Mr Jack Taylor.' And touched my face with one finger. It burned more than the spit of Cody's father.

I faltered, 'You mean like a date?'

She was at the door.

'No, I meant like consolation.'

'I don't need consolation.'

As she headed down the stairs she threw back, 'I wasn't talking about you.'

I was restless after she left, not knowing what to think. I picked up a book, opened it at random, read:

. . . if once a man indulges in murder, very soon he comes to think little of robbing, and from robbing, he next comes to drinking and Sabbath-breaking, and from that to incivility and pro-crastination . . .

The hell was this? Looked at the author: Thomas de Quincey.

Vinny, from Charly Byrnes's bookshop, had recently dropped me off a pile of books. A lot of them looked old and Vinny had said, 'Some of those volumes, the same age as yerself.'

I put the volume aside and figured the only one of that list remaining for me was procrastination. But if you factored in my total lack of dealing with whoever had shot Cody, I guess I had that pretty well covered too. I knew I should really be out there, giving my full attention to finding the shooter, but I was afraid. What if it was Cathy, Jeff's wife? I'd destroyed her daughter and husband, her whole life.

I took one of Gina's pills and waited, my mind in the dead place, and thought, 'These aren't worth a shite.'

Decided to lie down anyway, and slept for eighteen hours. If I had any dreams I don't recall them, but you can be sure they weren't the skip and jig variety. They never were.

The soaked-in-sweat sheets on my awakening testified to that. Business as usual.

As I'd slept, they were fishing Eoin Heaton's body out of the canal. His days of dog investigations were over.

16

*'If you carry a cross in your pocket,
no harm will come to you.'*

Irish priest in his sermon.

A local commented, *'It's not the cross in his
pocket we have to watch out for!'*

When I came to, the first feeling I had was relief that I hadn't drunk. Then I checked the clock and realized with alarm I'd been out for nigh on eighteen hours, and . . . I was hungry.

My right hand was throbbing, but not as bad as I'd expected. The guy in the alley, how would he be doing? I showered, made some kick-arse coffee and dressed in a white shirt, clean jeans and a tweed jacket I'd bought in the charity shop. It had leather patches on the sleeves, and if I had a pipe I could pass for a character out of a John Cheever novel or a professor on the skids. While I'd been shaving, I'd risked looking at my eyes in the mirror. They didn't reflect a killer, but then they rarely do. Murderous bastards I'd met – and I've met more than my share – had real nice eyes.

I briefly listened to the news and they mentioned a man found in an alley, victim of a mugging, who was in intensive care. Did I give a sigh of relief?

No.

Headed out, taking my by now usual walk up to the top

of the Square, to have a look at how the renovations were progressing.

They weren't.

And turning towards the city centre, walked past Faller's shop, stared with a pang of regret at the rows of gold Claddagh rings, then crossed the road and entered the Eyre Square Centre. They have a restaurant that still serves heart-attack food – fry ups, tons of cholesterol and no lecture. I ordered the special, the works, the whole clog-your-arteries mess: rashers, two fat sausages, black pudding, fried egg, round of toast, pot of tea. Got a table near the rear and was halfway through when my nemesis appeared.

Father Malachy.

He didn't ask to join me, just sat down, accused, 'Where have you been?'

I was mid bite of the second sausage so needed a second to answer. Malachy was, to pun heavily, fuming, as he couldn't smoke here. This was a lunatic who set the alarm to smoke in the small hours of the morning. Life for him was simply an irritation that occurred between cigarettes. He had the smoker's pallor, the heavy lined face and that slight wheezing that sounds almost like humming.

I decided to tell the truth, not something the Church was much accustomed to.

'I was sleeping.'

He was furious, spat, 'Sleeping it off, more like.'

I wasn't going to let the gobshite get to me. 'I'm not drinking.'

He snorted. It came out through his nostrils and was not

a pretty sound, especially when you're halfway through breakfast.

He said, 'You missed the funeral. That friend of yours was buried and you weren't bothered to even get your arse out of bed?'

I kept my voice level as I poured a cup of tea.

'I was asked not to attend.'

He let out a snigger of – delight?

'Well, by the holy – barred from a funeral, you're some beaut.'

I felt my tolerance slide, but no, he wouldn't get to me.

I asked, 'How did it go?'

He mimicked, '*Go?* The parents were crushed and his sister, the poor creature, was in bits.'

I was surprised, asked, 'He had a sister?'

He loved that.

'Jaysus, the poor lad worked with you and you didn't even know he had a sister. Isn't that just typical of Taylor, Mr Selfish, Mr couldn't care less.'

The temptation to bang him on the upside of his dandruffed head was building.

He noticed my bandaged hands.

'In the wars again?'

Took the cheap route, said, 'Yeah, a priest annoyed the shite out of me.'

He stood up, asked, 'Did you know that ex-Guard they pulled out of the canal?'

'What?'

'Fellah named Heaton. Drunkard like yourself. Did the world a favour and drowned himself.'

I was trying to take this in when he added, 'He didn't have to take the dog with him – that was really sick.'

'Dog?'

'The dirty yoke, he'd tied a dog to his stomach. What kind of perverted mind does that to one of God's gentle creations?'

So much for resolutions, Malachy had got to me in just about every way there is. I knew beyond a shadow of a doubt this was my fault. The dog-napping case had seemed so trivial. Now it was something completely different and I hadn't one clue what the hell was going on.

I spent the next few hours trailing round the pubs, the betting shops, the usual places Eoin Heaton would have frequented, and managed to discover that he'd been heading for a warehouse on Father Griffin Road the evening he'd died. He'd told one of his mates he was on the verge of solving a major scam.

Took me another few hours to find out the address of the place, and by then, when I got to it, it was closed. I had the name of the owner, though. A man called King.

Next, I rang Ridge from my mobile and she said she'd some information on Rory, the brother of the burned-car girl.

My mind was speeding. I had so much happening, and all at once, that I decided another good night's sleep was vital before I took action on all those cases.

Ridge came by early the next morning. Dressed in jeans and sweatshirt, she seemed almost relaxed. I noticed her eyes, they seemed a radiant blue and had a shine in them, and for once her clothes seemed just right. They not so much fitted her as blended into the whole air of confidence she was exuding.

For the first time in ages she took a full look at my place. In truth, it wasn't much. The sitting room, one battered sofa, the small television and, of course, the bookshelf, jammed with volumes. She checked the carpet – dust motes in every corner – then her eyes hit the small kitchen: the cups left in the sink, the dishcloth that badly needed to be thrown out, the packets of cereal way past their sell-by dates, and in the bin, takeaway cartons of fast food, pizza and Chinese, testifying to the lonely bachelor in all his shabby glory.

She crinkled her nose.

'Do I smell smoke? Are you smoking again?'

I snapped, 'Who are you, my mother?'

Before she could lash back, I softened with, 'Any new information?'

She told me what she'd learned.

The Willises' eldest son, Rory, had killed a woman in a hit and run, been arrested, got bail and skipped, to England, they thought. The woman he'd killed, Nora Mitchell, had two children in their late teens, early twenties, who had been living in Brixton. Her family were not reachable and Ridge said, 'They probably moved. Families often do after such a tragedy.'

All the sleep I'd been getting had me alert and – thoughts, ideas, hunches, whatever – my mind was getting crystal-clear pictures of a pattern. I waited a moment to put it together then dropped my bomb.

'Oh, they moved all right, and I think I know where.'

She paused.

'You're not suggesting her family are responsible?'

It was one of those rare moments, once every ten years, when I let my intuition act in unison with my experience.

I said, 'There's a connection, has to be.'

Ridge was highly sceptical, said, 'I'm highly sceptical.'

My mind was in hyperdrive and to stall I offered her coffee, then to rile her added, 'Or vodka?'

She looked like she was going to hit me.

'That was a one-off. And I'm off coffee, I don't need stimulants.'

Ignoring the mini lecture, I said, 'You'd need to get yer head out of yer arse is what you need.'

Her eyes danced in anger, but before she could reply I asked her about King, the warehouse guy, and told her about Eoin Heaton drowning in the canal.

She was vicious in her dismissal.

'Oh, for Christ's sake, he was a drunk, they go in the canal all the time, and if you ask me, not enough of them.'

I didn't rise to the taunt, asked, 'And what about the dog tied to his stomach?'

She gave a bitter, nigh twisted laugh, said, 'It's what drunks do, bring the innocent down with them.'

She was a piece of work.

I asked, 'Will you find out about King for me?'

'I'm not wasting time on a wild goose chase.'

Then I said, 'Maria Willis's funeral – I'm going to go.'

Ridge was horrified.

'God, how morbid are you? Why would you attend?'

'Call it a hunch.'

She looked like she might call it a lot of things, hunch not being one of them. She stormed past me, out the door.

I waited till she was in the hall, heading for the stairs and said, 'You're wrong.'

She didn't even look back. 'About what?'

'Geese. It's a dog chase. Get your terms of reference right.'

And I slammed the door.

Childish?

But very satisfying.

Back in the days of the Tinkers, when I'd worked with them, I'd met an English cop, name of Keegan. Now I've known crazy, been crazy, but he was so far out there, you'd have to invent a whole new order of madness. He'd been a great help to me and then, ignoring his advice, I'd made a tragic error of judgement. But we were friends and I called him.

Took a time to get him to the phone and his opening gambit was, 'Taylor, yah mad bollix.'

Same old greeting, same old banter.

We did the polite dance of asking for each other's health and all that stuff, then he went, 'So, whatcha want?'

Cut to the chase. I didn't bother feigning offence that he should think I was only calling for help, so I outlined the details of the crucifixion and asked him to check into the family of Nora Mitchell, anything he could get me.

He was quiet for a moment, then, 'You'll be wanting photos, rap sheets, if any, that sort of thing?'

'Exactly.'

'Have you a fax?'

I'd prepared for this, arranged with the local printers to receive and gave him the number.

He asked, 'What's in this for me, boyo?'

'My deep appreciation?'

'Fuck that, send me a case of Jameson.'

His parting words were, 'You're crucifying them now?'

What could I do but agree. He rang off with, 'You Catholics, you find a gig that works, you stick to it.'

Short of saying *We had it nailed*, I wished him luck. He said, 'Carry a Sig Sauer, luck won't matter.'

I paced my small room, all sorts of possibilities up for grabs. I wanted to make coffee but was too preoccupied to take the time to even boil a kettle.

Ridge rang to say that Mr King was a respected business-man who exported canned delicacies. He'd never been in trouble and was in every sense an upstanding citizen.

I asked, 'Fond of dogs, is he?'

She paused.

'What sort of silly question is that?'

'That's exactly what I intend to find out.'

I hung up on her protests.

The phone had exhausted me. When your hearing is wonky, it's a real strain and I felt knackered. Checked my calendar and wouldn't you know, it was my day to get fitted with the hearing aid.

I might not be able to see the full picture, but I'd certainly soon be able to hear the machinations behind it.

Told meself, I'd almost the makings of a Zen quote right there.

17

*'At the moment of commitment,
the universe conspires to assist you.'*

Goethe

The girl was planning to go to the funeral of the girl she'd burned.

Her father had cautioned against it, saying, 'They'll be right on this now. It can't be long till they figure it out.'

The girl wondered if he was losing his commitment. He was starting to look old and was always moaning about pains in his chest. What the fuck did he expect? They were killing people, did he expect to be uplifted? And her brother was a loser, whining as if he was born to it. Doing what he did best – like most men, sulking.

She said, 'We wanted them to suffer. What's the bloody point if we don't see it?'

Jesus, what was wrong with them?

Her brother said, 'I think we should keep a low profile.'

The girl stepped in, said in a cold measured tone, 'Rory, remember him?' She paused, making sure she had their full attention, then said, 'The one who mowed Mum down like an animal, who fled the scene, left her to die in agony by the side of the road. Are we going to let him dance away?'

They were suitably abashed.

Then her brother said, 'He won't come back, he'd be mad to.'

'His whole family have been wiped out. Even a pig like him will have to show.'

I got fitted with my hearing aid. It was smaller than I'd expected, less obtrusive, but still made me feel odd.

I asked the specialist, 'Does it show?'

He smiled.

'Depends on what you're looking for.'

A philosopher to boot.

I snapped, 'I don't want to seem like . . . you know, feeble.'

He laughed. 'I don't really think you can blame the hearing aid.'

Ireland, everyone feels they can speak freely, just lay it out. The fuckers never lie at the most crucial times. Save that for when you really need the truth.

I stared at him. He had a full head of hair so I asked, 'That a jig?'

He was horrified, tried, 'I'm not sure what you mean.'

'Sure you do. A jig . . . rhymes with wig.'

He touched his hair and said, 'It's my own hair.'

On my way out I said, 'Most people would believe you.'

When I saw the bill, I was very sorry about my flippancy.

The bandages were off my hands but you could see welts, bruises on the knuckles, and they hurt, but that was a familiar feeling. Ridge had given me some more info on King, the warehouse guy, and I put on my best charity-shop suit, added a white shirt and dark tie and I was good to go.

Though *good* is probably not the right term. More like antsy. I'd made up some documents. Between the internet and business centres, you could create just about any accreditation you wished for. I put mine in a small black leather case and practised flicking it open. I looked like a broken-down FBI agent and could only hope the hearing aid testified to gunfire.

King's warehouse was large and had an air of intense industry. Lots of vans coming and going. Business was brisk, but was it, dare I say, kosher? A receptionist in her early twenties greeted me warmly.

I flicked my ID, said, 'Department of Health. I wish to see Mr King.'

It's a constant source of amazement that any type of official document impresses people.

She was suitably impressed and said, 'I'll just buzz him, let him know you're here.' Then, with a worried frown, 'There's nothing wrong, is there?'

I kept my expression in neutral.

'That's what I'm here to find out.'

She spoke on the phone for a moment then announced, 'Mr King will see you now. Just go on through.'

I said, 'Don't leave town.'

Freud said, 'The most dangerous thing in the world is an angry baby.'

King looked like an angry baby, albeit a sixty-year-old one. He was completely bald, and seemed to have no eyebrows. There was not a line on his face, yet he had an air of having been round the block many times and each trip having been rough. He sat behind a massive desk and I bet he drove a massive car. He didn't rise to meet me, or offer his hand, just glared at me. I knew it wasn't personal, least not yet. Glaring was his gig. The world had his toys and, by Jesus, he was intent on getting them back.

I flipped the ID. 'Department of Health.'

He took a small container out of his impressive suit jacket, rammed snuff up his nose, least I think it was that. If it was coke, he had me full admiration. Then he did that irritating clearing of his nostrils and I waited.

He bawled, if you can do such a thing with a thin wispy voice, 'What's the problem?'

I sighed – always helps if you're weary too – said, 'We've had a complaint.'

He was on his feet, demanding, 'From whom? About what?'

I took out my notebook.

'I'm of course not at liberty to divulge our source, but I can tell you that some concern has been raised as to what you're exporting.'

He looked ready to explode.

'We export fish delicacies, sealed in tins. I just take delivery of the tins and send them on to our markets.'

I mused on this and then said, 'There's been a suggestion that something . . . erm, something other than fish is going into your product.'

He was on the verge of a major explosion.

'What the hell are you suggesting?'

I could have attempted to mollify him, ease him down a notch, but you know what, I didn't like the bollocks, he was an arrogant prick used to shouting and having tantrums, so I decided to push a little more.

'Our source mentioned you might be using . . . how should I put it . . . canine parts.'

Took him a moment to digest this and then he laughed. Not a sound like most laughter, more a mix of cackle and spite.

'I get it. Jesus H. Christ, that drunk who was here, a total burn-out, trying to say that dogs have been snatched and we're using them for our Asian markets.'

I fiddled with the hearing aid, trying to turn this guy down. He accused, 'Are you tuning me out?'

As if.

So I stayed with the needle, asked, 'And are you using such material?'

He seemed like he might physically attack me, but reconsidered and said, 'That's slander. What's your name again? I'll have your job for that.'

I kept my voice level, said, 'I haven't accused you of anything, simply posed a query. If you're clean, why are you bothered?'

He made a cutting gesture with his right palm, said, 'This charade is over. You want to talk to me again, contact my solicitor. Now get the hell out of my office.'

I stood up.

'Thank you for the coffee.'

Threw him, then he rallied.

'You're some kind of wise arse, that it? You won't be so

smug when I get your job reviewed. And that drunk, tell him to stay away from here.'

I said at the door, 'That might be a tad difficult.'

Always wanted to try *tad* in a sentence, see if it was as priggish as I thought.

It was.

He stopped his pacing, asked, 'Why, is he as deaf as you?'

I let that reverberate then said, 'No, he's dead. But I'll pass on your condolences to his family.'

Back in reception, the secretary was smiling and I saw a cheeky glint in her eye.

I said, 'Nice man, your boss. Must be a joy to work for.'

She looked back at his office. The door was closed and she whispered, 'Know what we call him? Crybaby.'

The fax had arrived from Keegan in London and I took it to a coffee shop, ordered a slice of Danish and double espresso, began to sift through the data.

Best of all, there were photos.

The father, Bob Mitchell, known as Mitch, was a small-time hood – some strong-arm stuff, credit-card scams, local enforcer, but nothing major. His son Sean was nineteen and there was something about the boy, I'd gotten a jolt of recognition, but couldn't pin it down. The daughter, Gail, was twenty, pleasant-looking face, nothing special.

Their mother, Nora, had been on holiday in Galway when she was killed by a hit-and-run driver.

Guess who?

Rory Willis, brother of the crucified boy. He'd been arrested, convicted and was waiting sentence when he skipped. In the old days, you got convicted, you went straight to prison, but now you had a time before sentence was handed down and usually you got time to prepare for your incarceration. It wasn't that we had such an enlightened justice system, it was pure maths – the jails were overcrowded and even convicted persons were out and around.

Rory was believed to have gone to England. Keegan had added his own thoughts: the family had been especially tight-knit and the girl had made some sort of suicide attempt after the death of her mother. The father had gone off the local radar and the whereabouts of the family was currently unknown.

My coffee came and I bit into the Danish. Very sweet but I appreciated the rush. Add the double espresso and my blood was hopping.

It had to be them, but the sheer violence of the two murders, a crucifixion and a burning, bothered me. There was a massive degree of insanity here that I couldn't fathom. Round and round it went in my head. The ferocity of their acts had me stumped, but it was them, wasn't it? And if it was?

Case solved.

My stomach heaved as the pictures, imagined, of what they'd done to that boy, the actual nails, etc. . . . Jesus.

Mainly I felt sickened to my stomach. Such violence, to crucify a boy, burn a girl in her car. I pushed the Danish aside. Even the coffee had lost all taste. The funeral, it came back to that. If I went, I was going to learn more, I was absolutely convinced.

Meanwhile I'd call Ridge, give her the material, see what she did with it.

As I said, just maybe I was finally getting a handle on this investigation lark. My instincts, free from the whispers, the dark warped whispers of cocaine, booze and nicotine, were finally kicking in.

Long time coming, oh yeah.

And more's the Irish pity it took so long.

My gut was telling me that Maria's funeral would bring the Mitchells out, certainly the girl. The more I read of Keegan's notes and faxes, the more I became certain she was the prime motivator, the dark angel. Proving for me that you throw enough grief at a person, wreak enough physical damage on a basic decent human being, you can create a monster. I was willing to bet my passage to America she'd show.

She did.

Wet doesn't describe the weather. As Bob Ward says, four kinds of rain, all bad. The real in-yer-face personal stuff, it wants to lash you, soak you to your soul, and by Jesus it does. Galwegians, they take rain as God's way of saying, 'I prefer the Brits.' I prepared for it: my Garda all-weather coat, Gore-Tex boots that I'd bought at a closing-down sale in a sports shop, an Irish fisherman's cap that I found in the flat.

It wasn't enough. Galway rain has ways of sneaking in, dribbling down the back of your neck, in your ears, and don't even mention the blinding assault on your eyes. My main concern was, would it affect the batteries in my hearing aid?

It didn't, but not from lack of trying.

A sizeable crowd for the funeral.

I spotted a girl dressed in a drab black coat, with a black beret to hide her hair, standing well back from the mourners, lest anyone chat to her. She was oblivious to the rain pelting her face.

I heard straight away that Maria's father had suffered a stroke and the mother had retreated into catatonia, and who could blame her?

This girl was bound to be feeling cheated, she wouldn't see their suffering. They were out of her game, and worse, there was no sign of Rory, the eldest son.

The burial went quickly and afterwards I approached her, said softly, 'Gail.'

I could see she thought it was a voice inside her head, but she turned and I knew she saw a middle-aged guy, with a slight smile and, OK, a bedraggled look. She was taken by surprise, the use of her name had thrown her.

'I'm Jack Taylor and yes, I know who you are. Come on, let me buy you a coffee.'

She marshalled her resources, dismissing me as some burned-out bum, despite what I said.

She said, 'I don't know you. Piss off.'

The steel in her eyes, I had no problem now imagining the acts she might have committed. I let my smile widen, gave a glance round the graveyard.

'Nice language in a cemetery, but here's the deal. See

these people, they're Claddagh folk, real clannish and they know me. You – not only are you English, I tell them you killed their kin, they'll tear you limb from limb.'

She risked a look round, and sure enough, some of the men were giving her hostile stares, nothing warm in their eyes.

She tried, 'You're bluffing.'

I spread my arms, palms opened. 'Try me.'

I grabbed her arm, said, 'I'll take that for a yes.'

I could see she wanted to lash out, but the truth was, she could sense the vibe in that place and she didn't want to test it.

She said, defiance writ large, 'I'm not paying for the coffee.'

I nodded, showing I was reasonable.

'Course not. But you'll be paying for all the rest. That's not a promise, that's a guarantee.'

There's a small café on the edge of the Claddagh, a no-frills place. They don't do lattes or any designer caffeine, they brew up huge pots of real strong java and if you don't like it, well, they couldn't give a fuck. We got in there, took off our sodden coats, sat and a woman in her late sixties came over and said, not asked, 'Two coffees?'

I nodded.

Gail asked, 'You have any apple tart?'

In the morning?

Go figure. She was English, I guess.

She looked at me and for one brief moment she was a young girl, almost naive. 'I love apple tart.'

A fleeting hint of a sweet nature and she got her mask back in place.

The coffee came and the tart, laden with cream, the woman saying, 'Nice young girl like you, deserve a treat.'

Yeah, nice . . . till she crucified a young man and burned his sister.

She dug into the tart, said between mouthfuls, 'I'd offer, but I'm not real big on sharing.'

I let that sit then said, 'I'm not real surprised.'

She finished it in jig time, wiped her mouth with a surprisingly gentle motion and gulped some coffee. She glanced briefly towards the corner of the café, as if she saw something there. Whatever it was, it seemed to embolden her.

Then she quickly looked back at me and asked in a harsh tone, 'So, fuckhead, what do you want?'

The change was instant. One moment Miss Dainty, and in the blink of an eye, psycho city.

I examined her face. She might have been pretty once, but the heavy make-up, the set of her jaw, neutralized that. Her eyes were the interesting feature. Nobody has black eyes in the literal sense, but she came as close as dammit. An energy came off her, like a blast from a furnace, and all of it malevolent. I moved back a few inches. You sit in the proximity of pure evil, it infects you.

I asked, 'What's next on the agenda? The elder brother doesn't show up, how are you going to pass the time? You have a taste for it now – killing people, I mean. You're not going to be able to stop, and you know what? You're not going to want to.'

This seemed to amuse her. She watched me with those black eyes, then shrugged.

'You know nothing about me.'

I wished I had a cigarette, it was definitely one of those times.

'What's to know? You're a sadistic bitch, a coward who went after easy prey. You think your mother would be proud of you? She'd spit on you.'

And the flash in the eyes, I saw the beast for one moment, deadly and lethal.

She leaned over, hissed, 'You bastard, you leave my mother out of this.'

I took a sip of my coffee, said, 'Your mother has nothing to do with this any more, you're doing this because you get off on it.'

Then her whole body language changed and she adopted a pose of lazy sensuality, stared into her already empty cup, purred, 'I want more coffee.'

Fucking with me, a terrain I was better able to play on.

I said, 'Get it yourself.'

She didn't, considered something, said, 'This has been interesting, but so what? You have no proof. If you could do anything, I'd already be under arrest. You're full of shit.'

No argument there.

'Justice isn't always in a courtroom,' I said.

She loved that, asked, 'You think you can take me on, a beat-up old geezer like you? You've a hearing aid, you walk with a limp, you couldn't find your dick with a map.'

Maybe it was the arrogance, or how much I detested that

guy who owned the warehouse, or just her virus rubbing off on me, but I suddenly decided to kill two birds with one stone. It seemed to strike me out of nowhere, and maybe that's how the worst things happen, spur-of-the-moment viciousness.

I said, 'It's not really me you have to worry about.'

Had her full attention and she asked what I meant.

I said in a slow measured tone, 'There's a man named King, owns a warehouse in Father Griffin Road, had a shine for Maria, and seemingly he has a way of proving you're the torch.'

I could see her literally mouthing his name, then, 'You tell him to stay the fuck out of my business.'

I was pleased to see I'd got to her, added some fuel.

'Nothing to do with me, but this guy has juice. Me, I'm nobody, like you said. But this fella, he has the means to see you get taken down.'

Her eyes closed for a moment and thank Christ I couldn't see whatever it was she was seeing.

She came back, said, 'I'm going now.'

I stared at her, she seemed almost ordinary.

Then, 'You stay the fuck away from me, Taylor, and who knows, I may lose interest in you.'

I held her stare, said, 'There's the catch, me girl. I have no intention of losing interest in you. In fact, next up, I'm going to have a chat with your brother. And I know where you live, did you know that?'

Her hand came up and only with supreme control did she rein it in.

'Sleep lightly, Taylor. Sometime, I'll be over your

bed, you'll wake up and you'll hear the sound of a match strike.'

I kept my face in neutral, said, 'I'll be expecting you. I might even get to show you the Irish version of a cross.'

She didn't get it, had to know, near spat, 'What the hell is that?'

'Oh, much like you did to the boy, with one difference.'

She raised her eyes in dismissive mode, asked, 'And that would be?'

'More nails.'

And she was gone, like some spectre that doesn't really belong to the daylight hours.

18

Cross that bridge when I come to it.

I went to the cemetery, feeling so guilty I hadn't attended Cody's funeral. And what to bring?

A little late for flowers and he wasn't really your flowers kind of kid. He'd been raving about the band Franz Ferdinand, so I bought one of their CDs, the assistant in the record shop telling me, 'They're past their best.'

Like I asked.

I wanted to add, 'Cody too.'

It was raining. Graveyards, I think they have a statute that rain is mandatory. As I walked among the crosses of the dead, I tried real hard not to read the inscriptions. I was carrying enough of the departed to keep a convent in perpetual prayer. Marvelled again that we're still the only burial ground with a Protestant and a Catholic side.

Up North, they wondered why the Peace Process was in shreds yet again and here, even the dead were divided.

I found the grave within five minutes, a small temporary marker simply with Cody's name and the date of his death. You're not allowed to erect a headstone for a year. Why? Like you're going to change your mind and go, 'I've had some time to reflect on it and don't think I'll bother with the memorial'?

The plot was a riot of flowers, mini statues of every saint in the calendar, tiny fluffy animals, well sodden from the rain already, and a framed photo of Cody. It didn't look like him and I was kind of relieved. It was a posed picture and you'd never have seen him still long enough for such a formal study. I never know the etiquette of graves. Do you kneel, pray, look forlorn as part of the deal, what?

I knelt.

Fuck it.

My pants dredging up the grass and dirt – be a bitch to clean – I placed the CD on the end and said, 'You could have been a contender.'

Said it in an American accent, he was real fond of that. I think I meant it, though like the best prayers it sounded hollow at the centre. Not the words, they were as good as any, but just phony.

I got to me feet, my knee aching and heard, 'Mr Taylor.'

Turned to meet Cody's mother. I'd only seen her the one time, when her husband spat in my face. She was dressed in a heavy black coat as dark as the shadows beneath her eyes. I nodded, truly lost for words.

She looked at the package I'd left and I said, 'A CD.' Feeling not only cheap but ridiculous.

She nodded, said, 'He loved music.'

Can a voice be tired, worn out?

Hers was.

She reached out and I flinched, expecting a lash. She touched my arm gently, said, 'He so admired you.'

Oh God.

I had to say it, feeble as it was.

'I'm so dreadfully sorry.'

She was staring at his photo, her eyes containing all the sorrow you'd ever see.

She said, 'You lose your child, life loses all meaning.'

Before I could mouth some awful platitude she added, 'You are a man who loss flows around.'

And for a horrible moment, I thought I'd lose it.

She added, 'I don't hate you, Mr Taylor, you gave our Cody a real sense of purpose for a little time.'

I wanted to say thank you but my voice had deserted me.

She continued, 'If I said my prayers any more, I'd even try to pray for you. But like me, I think you are beyond divine help.'

I've been cursed many times by experts, but few utterances have damned me like that. It was the quiet tone of utter conviction.

'Please go now, I want to be alone with my boy.'

As I shuffled away, I said to my own self, 'Dead man walking.'

I met with Ridge in Jury's Hotel, at the bottom of Quay Street. They'd a coffee bar that was priding itself on its class. That's the deal they were offering, and I don't know, don't think buying a coffee is going to endow you with class, no matter how much you pay for the damn stuff, but what the hell do I know. I ordered a double espresso but the machine was broken, so I had a Diet Coke.

Ridge arrived looking more together than of late. She

was dressed in a leather jacket, one of those short bomber jobs, and a skirt!

I stared at her legs and she gave me the look.

I said, 'What? You wear jeans all the time, I just wondered what you were hiding.'

She was angry, but being a woman, also curious. Asked, 'And . . . ?'

Being nice to her was always fraught, so I went with 'I've seen worse.'

She stared at my hearing aid and my bruised hands.

'This a whole new image? You're what, expecting them to do another remake of *Rocky*?'

I scowled at her, said, 'You're making jokes, drinking in the mornings – think you're having a mid-life crisis yer own self.'

I had given her the material Keegan had sent me from London and told her about my encounter with Gail. Now I asked, 'When will they arrest them?'

She looked away, didn't answer and I felt a surge of disbelief.

'You have everything you need, tell me they're going to act on it.'

She took a deep breath.

'It's all circumstantial, there's no hard proof and the feeling is that this English family suffered a bereavement in Ireland; to accuse them of these appalling crimes, without evidence, it would damage the tourist trade, affect relations between us and the UK and—'

I stopped her with 'Yeah, I know how it works, but for Christ's sake!'

I hadn't the words to vent my frustration. Sure, the system, as the Americans put it, *sucked*, but God Almighty, after me handing her the whole case on a plate, she must be able to do something.

I slammed my hand against my forehead in rage. I wanted to scream.

'I literally give this whole deal to you signed, solved and delivered, and what – nothing?'

Her face mirrored my consternation and I realized that blaming her was fruitless. I tried to let the rage burn off. All my life, God forgive me and with apologies to Eoin Heaton, I'd whipped the wrong dog.

I muttered, 'Aw, fuck it . . . fuck it all.'

'We'll be keeping a close eye. The official line is denial that any new leads have been found.'

Jesus, I was tired.

'You ever hear of Claud Cockburn?' I asked.

'Who?'

'He said, Never believe anything until it's officially denied.'

I had to ask.

'The tests, your, er . . . worry about your, er . . . health. Any word?'

She was amused at my hesitation to use the word *breast*, and it did me good to see her smile.

She said, 'I had a biopsy – not a pleasant ordeal – and they assure me they'll have the results soon.'

She was worried, added, 'But you, Jack, don't do anything reckless, OK?'

I looked round at Jury's, said, 'Me? No, I'll behave with class.'

Outside, I kicked a wall in frustration, and a guy passing quipped, 'Didn't win the Lotto, eh?'

City of fucking comedians.

Three days later, King's warehouse burned to the ground. The Guards came for me before noon, two of them, in uniform, with the new tunics, and of course the standard thick-soled shoes. Matched the expression in their eyes.

The first one, an older guy, said, 'The Super would like a word.'

The second one looked like he wanted to wallop me.

As I got in the squad car, I asked the older one, 'What's eating your partner?'

He shrugged. 'He doesn't like you.'

I looked at the guy, in his late twenties, full of spit and vinegar, the new breed, probably attended college at night.

'He doesn't even know me,' I said.

The guy laughed. 'Worse, he knows about you.'

I addressed the young gun. 'Don't suppose you want to tell me why you're bringing me in?'

He was a knot of suppressed anger, said, 'Shut your mouth.'

It's the Irish version of the Miranda deal.

They brought me straight to Clancy's office, the head honcho, the Super. My best mate once, we'd been on the beat together, learned the rudiments of policing. And then came my dismissal, my plummet down the toilet. And him, he rose through the ranks, slowly and surely. He was from

Roscommon, they know how to play the game and few knew how to play it like he did. Over the years, our relationship had become outright war. He pulled me in from time to time, tried to, if not neutralize me, at least intimidate me.

He was sitting behind a massive desk, his full dress blues, decorations on his chest like a riot of bad taste. His face had caved in, and deep lines were etched on every available patch of skin. I guess the game has its own price. He didn't look up for a moment from the array of papers on his desk, then snapped a folder shut, glanced up and said, 'Timmins, you can go.'

That was the older Guard. And to the young gun he said, 'You'll be sitting in with Mr Taylor and I.'

Clancy indicated the hard chair in front and for me to sit.

I did.

The young gun stood behind me.

I waited.

Clancy leaned back in his swivel chair, said, 'You've been stirring it again.'

I said, 'I'll need a little more to go on.'

A look passed between him and the young guy, and I knew who was the new hatchet man – the young guy, who obviously didn't like me. There's always one, the guy who'll do the dirty work, the follow-orders robot.

Clancy said, 'Mr King, a prominent businessman, a pillar of the community, his warehouse burned to the ground and it was no accident.'

I acted like I was mulling this over, then asked, 'And let

me hazard a guess, he's a member of the golf club, one of your buddies?'

I felt the young gun behind me stir, but resisted the impulse to turn round.

Clancy ignored that, continued.

'A few days ago, a Department of Health official visited him, a man who bears a striking likeness to you and makes thinly veiled threats. And prior to this, an alkie, a disgraced ex-Guard, also made similar threats. What the two had in common was a wild-arse theory that Mr King was stuffing his merchandise with dog parts.'

The guy behind me guffawed, there is no other description for it.

Clancy waited for my response, but I simply stared at him.

Then he asked, 'What are you now – pet detective? It's not enough you kill a child, cause the death of an innocent young man, now you hassle the solid citizens?'

I forced myself to let the comments slide and asked, 'Am I under arrest?'

He stood up.

'We've been in touch with the Department of Health, and if they want to press charges, we'll be happy to oblige. Meanwhile, a word to the wise – stay the hell away from Garda business. You want to investigate something, why don't you find out who shot the young man whose care you were responsible for?'

I had to grit my teeth. 'Oh I will.'

He came round the desk and leaned in real close. His aftershave was expensive, if overpowering.

'We already did, and you know what? Surprise, surprise, it was the mother of the little girl you killed.'

I tried not to show my amazement. 'So, did you arrest her?'

He straightened up, shook some lint off his shoulders. 'Soon as we locate her. Thing is, we're kind of hoping she might make another attempt and we can catch her in the act, after she's done the . . . dirty deed.'

And then he was gone.

Before I could stand up to leave, the young guy hit me on the ear with a powerhouse, the blow knocking me from the chair and dislodging my earpiece. He brought his heel down on it, ground it, then bent and shouted, 'Can you hear me, arsehole? Stay the fuck away from Guard affairs.'

I heard him.

19

'Not knowing how near the truth is,
we seek it far away.'

Hakuin

The Americans have an expression for verbally attacking someone. When you want to really lash into someone, they say, *tear 'em a new asshole.*

I tore one for Ridge.

Like this.

'The fuck when you were going to tell me about Cathy Bellingham?'

I'd asked – no, amend that, I fucking ordered her to meet me in the Great Southern Hotel and slammed down the phone.

I got there first, went to the end of the lounge, under the bust of James Joyce, stared at him, near shouted, 'The fuck are you looking at?'

Yeah, you're screaming at a bronze head of one of Ireland's most famous writers, you've either gone completely mad or just heard you lost the Booker Prize.

The porter approached. He and I had history, most of it bad, and he ventured, 'Long time no see, Jack.'

His voice was quiet, as if he wasn't yet sure if I was drinking. If I was, he was heading for the hills. As I said, history.

I sat down, levelled dead eyes at him. 'Help you with something?'

He gave a nervous laugh. 'Actually, those are my lines. I'm the one who works here.'

Keeping it light, as if we were just a couple of old mates having a touch of merry banter.

I said, 'So go work, you see me preventing you?'

He looked round – for help?

None was forthcoming so he asked, 'I, er, wondered if I could get you something – tea, coffee?'

'Get out of my face, you could get me that.'

He did.

Ridge arrived, dressed in smart new suede jacket, tight jeans and those pointy-toed boots that have to be murder. The porter had a word with her and I could see her nodding, so I figured he'd warned her I was not exactly mellow. I don't think this was a surprise to her. She walked over, a purpose in her stride, like she wasn't going to take any shite from me.

'Yeah?'

I launched in straight away. She reeled for a moment then asked, 'How did you find out about Cathy Belling-ham?'

Cathy . . . Oh God, our long and tortuous history. We'd met originally when she washed up in Galway from London. She'd just kicked heroin, was a real punk, had lived the life. She sang like an angel and had a tongue like a fishwife. We hit it off immediately. She'd helped me on a number of cases, then I introduced her to my best friend, Jeff, and damn it all to hell, they jelled, got married and had the little girl with Down's Syndrome, Serena May. She sure had reason to want me dead.

'Clancy told me. Remember him, your boss?'

She savoured that then said, 'Her apartment was searched and bullets were found that matched the rifle, the . . . er . . . weapon . . . used.'

She was treading delicately round the use of Cody's name. I could understand that, I found it difficult to utter his name too.

'And where is she now, apart from lining up another shot at me?'

Ridge put her head down, muttered something.

I'd been able to get the earpiece repaired. Despite the Guard's stomping, he'd only managed to crack the casing. Hardy little suckers those – the earpiece, that is.

I adjusted the volume and said, 'Speak up.'

'We don't know.'

I sat back, let that sit between us, then said, 'What an outfit. I give you enough proof to arrest a family of psychos, and you do nothing. You have evidence to arrest the person who tried to shoot me, and you can't find her. How are you guys doing with traffic these days?'

She said the worst thing. 'I understand your frustration.'

I jumped up – well, jumped in so far as a bad leg allows – said, 'Like fuck you do.'

And stormed out.

I needed to do something, so I concentrated on the weak link of the murderous family: the brother, Sean.

According to the information Keegan had sent, his only

interest seemed to be music, so I began a stake-out of the record shops, places where they sold musical instruments. Boring, frustrating work, but I had nothing else to do.

Three days of this tedium and I was about to pack it in, when I thought I spotted him. Just off Dominic Street, going into a secondhand shop that sold guitars. He was admiring one hanging on the wall when I came up behind him.

'Nice instrument.'

He whirled around. 'I know you?'

And suddenly the photo clicked into place, the nagging feeling I'd had that I knew him. He was the grunge kid, the Kurt Cobain lookalike from the coffee shop in the Eyre Square Centre.

His eyes suddenly brightened, he remembered me too.

He tried to brush past me and I grabbed his arm, not gently, I could feel the stick-thin sinew, and squeezed.

'Hey, that hurts.'

A burly guy manning the counter raised his head and asked, 'Is there a problem?'

I said to Sean, 'I've spoken to your sister. You want me to tell the guy about the crucifixion or you want to come have a coffee with me? We can talk about your band.'

He pulled his arm loose and headed out.

I looked at the counter guy, indicated the guitar, said, 'It's only rock and roll.'

Sean was standing outside. A slight bead of sweat was forming on his brow, yet he was rubbing his hands as if he were cold.

I said, 'The Galway Arms, they do good coffee, and

who knows, you behave yourself, might have a sticky bun.'

As we began to walk he said, 'I don't like sweet things.'

Christ, I nearly laughed.

The owner of the place gave me a warm greeting and Sean sneered, 'Know everybody, doncha?'

His accent was much more Brixton than his sister's. Her tone had acquired a sophisticated veneer. I suppose if you reinvent yourself, a change of accent is the least of your problems.

I said, 'Thing is, pal, I know you.'

The owner brought over a pot of coffee and some cups and said, 'Enjoy.'

Sean waited till the guy had gone, then said, 'You don't know me.'

He took out a pack of roll-ups and some tobacco and began to build one.

'You can't smoke, it's the law. You've been here long enough to learn that.'

He stuffed the tobacco in his jacket, said, 'Stupid fucking law.'

I smiled. 'And of course the law doesn't apply to you or your family, right?'

I poured the coffee, looked at him. He had the body language of a beaten dog, living his life waiting for the next blow and rarely waiting long. And I was just one more in a long line of beaters. His face was riddled with acne and his lips were sore, cracked from his nervous licking of them. He had delicate hands. Who knows, maybe he could have been a musician. Wasn't going to happen now.

'I don't think your heart is in this . . . gig. You're being
swept along, and guess what? When the shite hits the fan,
which it will and real soon, guess whose arse will be in the
sling? It sure as hell isn't going to be your sister, she's way
too smart for that.'

He lifted his cup, a shake in his hand, made a slurping
sound, more like a groan, and then said, 'I'm not afraid of
you.'

He was. And not just me, everything that walked the
planet. Just one of the world's natural victims. I almost felt
sorry for him.

Almost.

I said, 'Not me you have to be afraid of. In fact, I might
be the only hope you've got.'

He attempted some hard, had probably waited his whole
life to attempt it, made a feeble effort at a snigger. 'Yeah,
right.'

Time to rattle his cage. His one shot at bravado and I
was about to smash it.

'One of two things in your future. You either get caught,
or you carry on looking for the elusive brother your family
are so desperate to find. Rory, that's his name, right? You
probably know the answer to that better than me, but
pretty it won't be. We can agree on that, right? When I had
my little chat with your sister, I didn't get any sense of
fraternal affection.'

He was staring at me. 'I dunno what fraternal means.'
Jesus.

I sighed. Demolishing this kid was not the simple task it
had first presented. Christ, he was like a puppy on a busy

road, hoping a car would stop and take him in. I continued, though I had lost any zeal for it.

'Or you go to prison. And a kid like you, the long hair,
the weak-as-shite personality, they'll run a freight train
through yer arse before supper, and that's just for openers.'

Hard to say which scenario freaked him more. His body
gave a shudder and he said, 'I want to go home, that's all.
Just leave.'

No protestations of innocence, no argument about me
being wrong, no fight at all.

I said, 'Not going to happen, kid.'

He began to weep. I could have taken anything – any-
fuckingthing – but that. I nearly reached out to him, and
then what?

I let him cry it out then I said, 'Give it up. I'll help you,
get the best deal that's going.'

He dabbed at his eyes, then said, 'I need a smoke.'

I left some notes on the table and followed him outside.
He didn't wait, started to move away and I followed.

'What's it going to be, kid? You with me? This is it,
make-up-your-mind time.'

He stopped, turned, gave me a look of such agony that I
had to glance away, and then he said, 'I can't, they'd kill
me.'

'They'll kill you anyway.'

He looked up at the street, terror in his eyes, but I
couldn't see anybody. He said, 'I hope so.'

When I finally got home I was bone tired, but not too
exhausted to miss the smell of smoke. I cautiously entered

my tiny sitting room. All my books had been piled in a heap, set on fire and were smouldering nicely.

I went to the bathroom, filled a basin with cold water and doused my prized possessions.

Then I noticed the table. It had one of those toy cars, it had also been burned, and I could see a tiny stick figure in the front seat, burned but still recognizable. Meant to be a girl, I'd hazard. And underneath the tiny car was a note:

> Hot enough for you?
> Gail

The fucking bitch.

And then, in one of those odd moments of madness, I thought, 'Girl, you sure saved me from having to decide what to do with the books. With my going to America, I wasn't sure which volumes to bring. That's solved now.'

But rage was building. She'd not only come to my home, but taken the one thing that still had any meaning. Books have been the only reliable, the only comfort zone I had left, and I swear, the bloody demented psycho, she knew, she fucking knew how to hit me.

Took deep breaths, tried to see myself on that plane in a month's time, all of this behind me. Didn't ease the storm of pure hatred I felt and I swore, 'I'll bring you down before I leave, girl, I swear by all that's holy, if it's the very last thing I do. I'm going to put a halt to your insane gallop.'

20

'A cross offers two options: you can be nailed to it . . . or lie on it, as a voluntary act.'

Irish saying

I needed protection.

Chances were that Gail would take another pass at me and a more serious one. I better be ready, and if I was going to take on the whole family, at least Gail and her father, I'd need more than an attitude. You want to buy a gun in Galway these days, you are spoiled for opportunity. So many different nationalities here that weapons have become more and more common. You frequent the pubs, the back streets, it doesn't take long to find out where to score dope, hookers, whatever you fancy.

I went to a pub in Salthill, not a place I'd go to by desire. It's off the main strip and looks seedy. It is seedy, and has gained a new rep as the place to buy and sell . . . anything.

An East European named Mikhail, who depending on the day was Russian, Croatian, Romanian and other nationalities I couldn't pronounce, held court at a table by the window. In a month's time he'd move somewhere else, but by the ocean was the venue for now. I knew him, if not well, at least well enough that when I asked 'Buy you a drink?' he agreed.

He had that buzz-cut hair we used to call a crew cut, a long face pitted with scars, and eyes that held no expression at all. He was thin to the point of starvation and his age was in that zone between late forties and very bad fifties. He said a shot of vodka would be most welcome. I got that and a Diet Pepsi for meself, sat at the table.

He looked at my drink, asked, 'You no drink Coca-Cola?'

The fuck did he care?

I said, 'I'm on a diet.'

He surveyed my hands. The cuts and bruises were healing but still visible, and he asked, 'You a street-fighting man?'

When I bought the gun, maybe I'd shoot him.

'Not by choice.'

Right answer. He loved it, laughed out loud, exposing a mouth of rotten teeth with flecks of – gold? – in there. I'd ensure not to amuse him further.

'Ess a song by the Rolling Stones. You love this, yes?'

Sure, my favourite.

I said, 'My favourite.'

More laughter, fuck, and he accused, in easy fashion, 'You make joke with me, am I right?'

And I was smart enough to add, 'But not at you.'

He nodded. No doubt about it, we were made for each other.

Then he knocked back the vodka in one fell swoop, asked, 'What I can get you, Mr Street-Fighting Man?'

I leaned in close, said I needed a gun.

His mobile phone rang but he ignored it, said, 'Please, to come to my office.'

I followed him outside, and up beside Salthill church.

He'd a battered van, unlocked it, asked, 'Please to join me.'

We got in and he reached in the back, took out a heavy bundle wrapped in cloth and unfolded it to reveal a Glock, a Beretta and a Browning Automatic. Guns R Us. That his business was right beside the church seemed to make a sort of new Ireland twisted sense.

I asked, 'Aren't you afraid of the van being stolen?'

He exposed those teeth again and I swear snarled, went, 'Who is going to steal from me?'

As if I had inside information.

To distract him, I asked the price of the Glock and it was expensive.

I said, 'It's expensive.'

He shrugged, as in *Tell me about it.*

With a full round of ammunition, it was more than I'd expected to pay, but what the hell, it wasn't like I could use the Yellow Pages.

I asked, 'How do you know I'm not a policeman?'

Huge laugh. 'You?'

I didn't ask him to elaborate.

He indicated my earpiece.

'You no hear so good?'

'I hear what's important.'

That intrigued him.

'How you can tell the difference?'

I couldn't, but decided to shine him on.

'It's not what's being said, but how the person saying it is acting.'

A crock, right?

But he bought it big time, said, 'This I like. May I please to use this?'

Jesus.

I said, 'Knock yourself out.'

Got another mega laugh. Maybe I should go live in Eastern Europe, become a stand-up.

I said, 'Thanks for your time.'

He put out his hand and we shook.

He said, 'I like you, Meester, you make me laugh. This country, it don't make me laugh so much.'

At the risk of sounding like a Zen master, I went for 'You're looking at it the wrong way.'

He considered, then asked, 'And how is, how is to look at it?'

'As if it doesn't matter.'

Not really grasping that, he probed, 'And does it matter?'

I got out of the van, finished with, 'Soon as I find out, I'll let you know.'

I also needed somebody to talk to.

Before, I'd always just forged ahead, ignoring advice, making it up as I went along. And of course, I'd been drinking. Who needed advice? I had the booze giving me all the crazy suggestions I could handle.

Sober now, or dry, whatever, maybe it was time to get some help. Ridge was out. We were so locked in combat she wouldn't be any assistance, and if she knew I'd bought a gun, she'd probably arrest me.

Jeff, my great friend, was MIA. Since I'd caused the death of his child, he'd vanished off the face of the earth. All my efforts to locate him had failed.

And that was it. To get to my age and have no one, not one soul to confide in, it's a crying shame and testament to how much my way of life had cost me. I toyed with the idea of giving Gina a call. I definitely felt something for her. I no longer knew what love was – if I ever had – but till I sorted out the family of killers, I decided to wait.

Which left Stewart, the drug-dealer. Instead of analysing it to death, I just called him and he said, 'Come by, I've just bought some new herbal tea.'

I could only hope the tea was a joke.

I stopped in a religious shop en route. There's one near the Augustinian church: lots of relics of St Jude, spanking new books on the late Pope. I couldn't find what I was looking for, just like U2.

The woman behind the counter said, 'I know you.'

Like the theme song of me life.

And never uplifting.

She said, 'I knew your mother.'

I waited for the usual homilies, platitudes, the dirge about her being so holy, damn near a saint and all the other horseshite. I nodded, thinking, Let's get the beatification over with.

She said, 'Hard woman, your mother, but I don't suppose I have to tell you that.'

I warmed to her instantly, asked, 'Have you a St Bridget's Cross?'

She smiled, a smile of real warmth.

'By the holy, we don't get much demand for those any more.'

But said she'd check the storeroom.

I read a plaque of the Desiderata while I was waiting, and figured with that and the Glock, you were set for life's setbacks.

The woman had one cross, blew some dust off it and said, 'There's no price on it.'

I handed over a twenty-euro note and she said it was far too much. I told her to put it in the poor-box.

She allowed herself another smile.

'Oh, we don't call them that any more, we say *the disadvantaged.*'

I had no reply to this, thanked her for her time.

As I left, she said, 'God mind you well.'

I sure as hell hoped someone would. I was doing a bad job of it me own self.

When Stewart answered his door I didn't recognize him for a moment, then realized he'd shaved his head.

I said, 'You're really taking this Zen gig to the limit.'

He motioned me in.

'I'm losing my hair. This way, I don't have to see it happen piecemeal.'

Argue that.

It gave him a hard-arse look and, coupled with the new stone eyes, totally changed him from the bank-clerk type I'd first encountered those years ago. The whole vibe cautioned, 'Don't fuck with me.'

The flat was still spartan and held an air of vacancy.

He said, 'I'll get the tea.'

Yeah.

I sat wondering if I could score some more of those magic pills.

He came back with two mugs of some vile-smelling stuff, put it in front of me, asked, 'What's on your mind, Jack?'

I moved back from the mug and tried for levity. 'I can't just drop by for a social call?'

He shook his head, took a sip of his tea. 'You don't do social, Jack, so what's on your mind?'

What the hell? I told him. All of it – the family who killed as a unit. Took time to lay it all out.

He listened without interruption, and when I finished, I almost took a taste of the tea. Then I remembered the present, took it out of my pocket, said, 'House-warming token.'

He was surprised, opened it and said, 'You bring me a cross – you don't think I've enough of a burden?'

Didn't sound like gratitude.

'It's good luck, keep your home safe.'

He put it aside, said, 'Take more than St What's Her Name to achieve that.'

I was a bit put out.

'Those crosses are hard to get.'

Jesus, sounded lame even as I said it.

He finished his tea, said, 'So is luck.'

Before I could reply, he asked, 'What are you planning to do?'

'I've no idea.'

He let that float around, then said, 'It's fairly simple. I've been reading Thich Nhat Hanh, who said, "Don't just *do* something. Sit there."'

Just what I needed, philosophy.

I asked, 'You're saying I should do nothing?'

He stood up, flexed his body in some sort of yoga movement.

'I'm saying, kill the sister.'

I'd hoped for some brilliant idea, some radical scheme that would solve everything and, in truth, let me off the hook. So I could walk away, go to America and have, if not a clear conscience, then at least some tiny measure of ease.

Wasn't going to happen.

I raised my hands in a futile gesture, meaning 'That's the best you can do?'

He reached in his pocket, took out a tube of pills and threw it to me.

'You'll be wanting these.'

I wanted to protest, get indignant, fling them back, exert some dignity, but I wanted the pills more.

'Thanks.'

He shrugged, asked, 'You want help?'

Did he mean with my growing addiction?

He said, 'You'll need to know where the enemy lives, and let's face it, I can do that better than you, I still have all my network.'

Ridge wasn't going to help me, and tramping around on me own, hoping to get lucky, that wasn't too smart, so I said, 'Yeah, I'd appreciate that.'

He smiled, actually a hint of warmth in this one.

'You don't like relying on people, do you, Jack?'

Not a whole lot of mileage in lying so I said, 'No. No, I don't.'

He moved over to a small press, rummaged in there, took out a CD, frowned at it, then said, 'And when I find them, and find them I will, you want me to come do the deed with you?'

The deed?

Before I could mouth some crap about needing to do this alone, he said, 'My sister was murdered, and you helped me. These . . . *people* . . . wiping out a whole family, I feel I could get some closure by blowing out their candle.'

I had to ask, 'Stewart, you do know what you're saying?'

He'd come to some decision on the CD.

'I always know what I'm saying – that's why I say so little.'

Deep.

I stood up, didn't know if I should shake his hand, seal the pact, but he was offering the CD.

'This is for you. You give me a cross, here's something similar back, though perhaps a bit easier to carry.'

It had a black cover, which was appropriate. The title was *I've Got My Own Hell To Raise*, by someone called Bettye LaVette.

I indicated the title, asked, 'Cryptic message to me?'

He was moving me towards the door, said, 'It's a CD. Not everything has significance.'

I gave him my mobile number and he said, 'You'll be hearing from me, so keep the hearing aid on.'

Yeah.

21

'When you eat, the meal is yourself.'

Zen saying

Ed O'Brien, the dog guy – the man who hired me to investigate the stolen canines – I felt I better make a report to him. What to tell him? That I'd hired an alkie ex-cop who ended up in the canal? That I was fairly sure a businessman named King was putting the dogs in tins and I'd set a psycho to burn the warehouse to the ground?

Some report.

Whatever else, I'd surely have his full attention.

He'd given me his address. It was in Newcastle Lower, right alongside the university, and the walk there is almost soothing. You can hear the roar of the students, the high-spirited laughter and the sheer buzz of life. I found the house without any bother, one of those ivy-covered jobs, you have to figure a professor of something serious lives there. A heavy iron gate and then a short walk to the main door. Large neglected garden. When you're rich, you can afford to do neglect, it adds to the allure. A sign on the door warned:

No salesmen

All I was pitching was trouble and strife. I rang the door, waited, and finally it was opened by O'Brien, dressed in one of those heavy Aran cardigans I thought only the Americans purchased, and brown corduroy pants that were misshapen to the point of ridicule. He had a heavy book in his hand.

He stared at me, said, 'Can't you read the sign?'

I knew it had been a time since he'd enlisted my help, but not that long.

I said, 'I'm Jack Taylor.'

The penny dropped and he took a moment, as if he was going to dismiss me, then he said, 'I suppose you'd better come in.'

Suppose?

I could tell this was going to be a beauty.

We entered a book-lined study, with comfortable worn furniture and a walnut writing desk, a riot of papers and folders on top. He settled himself behind it, indicated a hard chair in front. I sat, feeling like I was about to be interviewed.

I wasn't sure where to begin, but he said, 'To tell you the truth, Taylor, we thought you'd never bothered.'

A factory burned to the ground, a dead man pulled from the canal – imagine if I'd *bothered*.

I said, 'I didn't want to get back to you till I had something to report.'

His face conveyed total scepticism and I had a building desire to swipe the smirk off his face.

He shook his head, as if he'd met every sort of con man and I was just one more in a pathetic line. He confirmed this by saying, 'You're here to get paid, I expect.'

It had been the last thing on my mind, but before I could get this out, he said, 'You think because the affair is solved you'd, what? Come waltzing in and try and claim a fee? I wasn't born yesterday, Taylor.'

Solved?

I echoed, 'Solved? What are you talking about?'

He mocked, 'The case is solved and ace investigator Taylor doesn't even know it. I think you might consider a new line of work, you're not exactly up to speed with this one.'

Seeing my blank face, he realized I truly didn't know, and said with an exaggerated patient tone, 'A gang of teenagers were snatching the dogs, bringing them to the waste ground beside the hospital and dousing them with petrol, then seeing how far they could run before they – how shall we put it – *burned out*?'

'Jesus.'

He rubbed his hands together as if he were dry-washing and said, 'I doubt the Lord had anything to do with it, save perhaps in His mighty wrath.'

The last words carried a ring of fundamentalism that was as chilling as it sounds.

'It wasn't in the papers – I didn't hear it on any news bulletins.'

Now he smiled, and there was a hint of mania, just a small dribble of spit on his lower lip, a sheen of excitement in his eyes.

'The powers that be are too busy to deal with something as mundane as missing dogs. Why, you yourself didn't think it worth your time to even make a lazy attempt at checking into it. The world is gone to hell, Taylor. If you were ever sober for any length of time, you might have noticed.'

I was clenching my fists, trying not to go over to the desk.

He continued, 'So we began a more active style of Neighbourhood Watch, and let me say, those particular teenagers won't be stealing dogs – or indeed anything else – for some time. Do I need to spell it out for you?'

He nigh glowed with his self-righteousness.

I said, 'Vigilantes, that's what you are.'

He stood up. My session was over.

'Ah, Taylor, we are what this city needs, citizens of affirmative action.'

Short of walloping the bejaysus out of him, there was no way of bursting his smugness. I said, 'The Klan have a similar line of rhetoric. You wear sheets yet?'

He looked at me with complete contempt.

'Goodbye, Taylor, and let me add, you're not welcome in this neighbourhood, we're trying for decency and respect-ability here.'

Fucker was threatening me. I asked, 'Or what, you'll take affirmative action?'

He opened the front door, said, 'Treat it as a friendly word of caution.'

'I'll walk wherever I damn well like, and you decide to take affirmative action, bring more than a sheet with you, pal.'

I headed down towards the canal, bile in my mouth and deep regret that I hadn't taken at least one pop at him. My mind was a maelstrom. King's factory had been razed for nothing, and Eoin Heaton drowned in the canal. Why?

A woman carrying a charity box, selling flags for the homeless, approached.

'Would you like to help the poor?'

I fumbled for a note, shoved a twenty in the box, said, 'Wrong terminology.'

She stared at me. 'Excuse me?'

'The poor. I'm reliably informed they're now the disadvantaged.'

She moved away quickly, keeping the twenty.

I went back to Eoin Heaton's haunts, trying to figure out what the hell happened to him. A round of dingy pubs, dire bookies' offices and hit if not pay dirt, at least a lead in the Social Security Office – a guy there told me Heaton had lived with his mother, and if anyone knew him, she did.

She lived in Bohermore, in one of the few remaining original houses that hadn't been converted to a townhouse. The original one-up, one-down model, in a terrace. It had a tiny garden that was well tended and the front had been freshly painted.

I knocked at the door and it was opened by a tiny woman, bent in half by age and poverty. Her clothes were spotless, clean as anything to emerge from the Magdalen Laundry. The memory of that place gave me a shudder.

'Mrs Heaton, I am so sorry to bother you, I was a friend of Eoin's.'

She lifted her head with obvious effort, looked at me, said, 'Come in, *amac* (son).'

Jeez, I hadn't heard that term in twenty years. She led the way into a small sitting room, again clean as redemption. The wall had three framed pictures: the Pope, the Sacred Heart, and Eoin in his Guard uniform. He looked impossibly young, fresh-faced and with an eagerness that tore at my heart.

Mrs Heaton asked, 'Can I get you a drop of tea, loveen?'

Jesus.

Loveen.

Time was, this term of endearment was as common as muggings. You never heard it any more. It conveyed effortless warmth and an intimacy that was reassuring without being intrusive. For one insane moment, I thought I was going to weep. I said I'd love a cup of tea. The old ritual, also dying out. Nowadays you went to a house, you got offered designer coffee and no warmth, maybe a stock option to put on the tray with the flash caffeine. You'd never refuse tea from such a lady, it would be like spitting in her face. And no matter how old or fragile she was, you never – ever – offered to help.

On the mantelpiece – which was covered with Irish lace, all hand embroidered – were trophies for hurling and Gaelic football, and a small bottle of Lourdes holy water. I took out one of Stewart's pills and swallowed it. I was more shaken than I wanted to admit.

Five minutes later, she returned with a tray. A pot of tea, her best china and a slab of fruitcake.

She raised her head, asked, 'Would you like a drop of the creature?'

Whiskey.

Only if I could never leave and finish the whole bottle.

'No, the tea will be grand.'

Slipping into the old way of talking as if I'd never left.

She said, 'We'll let the tea draw.'

She lowered herself with deliberate movement into an armchair, and used a spoon to stir the pot. Around her neck was a Miraculous Medal, held by blue string.

She said, 'Isn't it fierce cold?'

It wasn't.

I said, 'It's bitter.'

Tea and the weather, does it get more Irish?

I said, 'I'm so sorry about Eoin.'

Fuck, I tried to come up with some convincing lie about him, but she was his mother, she was going to believe any crumb I could dredge up.

I tried, 'He was a good man.'

Brilliant, just fucking inspired.

She began to sob. Not loudly – worse, those silent ones that rack the frame. A tear ran down her cheek, hit the china cup, made a soft plink, and I knew, knew with every fabric of my being, it would join the phantom orchestra of nightmarish melodies that tormented my sleep.

She dabbed at her eyes with a tissue, said, 'I'm sorry, Mr Taylor, it's . . .'

I rushed in with, 'Please, Mrs Heaton, call me Jack.'

She wouldn't, but it bought me some time. I asked, 'Is there anything I can do? Get you?'

She shook her head. 'Eoin was . . . very troubled, and the drink, that is a fierce curse, he couldn't get free of it.'

I was trying to think of a way to get out when she said, 'I didn't think he'd bring Blackie.'

Like a complete moron, I echoed, 'Blackie?'

As if she was talking to herself, she continued, 'Of course, he loved that dog, and I should have known he'd never leave without him.'

I felt my mind whirl, dance and reel as I attempted to put this into perspective.

'Blackie was his dog?'

The shrewd detective, not missing a beat, right on top of the data.

She gave a small smile, it lit up her whole lovely face, took thirty years straight off her.

'He lived for that animal, and when he . . . he . . . went into the river, I wasn't surprised he took Blackie.'

She fumbled in her apron, took out a neatly folded sheet of paper, offered it to me.

'He left this for me.'

With a sinking heart, I took it, unfolded it, read:

My Dear Mamie
   I'm so sorry, I can't go on and please pray for me, I'm bringing Blackie for company, there's a few hundred euro in my sock drawer. I love you Mam.
         XXXXXXX Eoin

I handed her back the note, unable to say a single word.

She said, 'He used his belt to tie Blackie to him. It was his Guards one, he was fierce proud of that. When they

222

took his uniform, he held on to the belt. Do you think they'll take it back?'

'No . . . No, they won't.'

I got up to leave, promised I'd call in from time to time, check on her.

She said, 'You never ate your cake. Wait a minute.' And she went to the alcove, wrapped it in paper, said, 'That will be nice after your dinner. A growing man like yourself, you need something sweet for energy.'

She reached up and gave me a hug.

After I got out, I walked down the street in a daze, the slice of cake in my hand like the worst kind of recrimination.

The pub beckoned stronger than in a long time, but the odd thing, I felt it would be a real slap in the face to Mrs Heaton to use her grief to fuel my own desperation. I was guilty of so many things, but adding her to the list, that I couldn't quite stretch to.

I swallowed another of Stewart's pills.

22

'A thirsty evil; when we drink we die.'

Shakespeare

Gail was about to leave the club when the man spoke to her.

He said, 'Buffy the Vampire Slayer?'

She'd heard every line in the book, but this caught her. The guy was older than most of the other clubbers, but she could see he was in shape, a tight lean body. But the eyes, the eyes were the lure. Hard, cold, like she knew she had her own self. He was wearing jeans, and a white open-neck shirt that showed off his build.

She said, 'Is that, like, a line?'

He shrugged. 'I'm sitting over there, having me some tequila shots. You want to do some?'

She loved tequila, got you there in jig time. He didn't wait for an answer, just moved on and sat down. That appealed big time. Usually guys were whinging, pleading with her to join them. This one, he acted like he couldn't care less.

She went and sat opposite him. A row of shots were lined on the table. She asked, looking around at the dancers, 'Aren't you afraid someone will steal your drinks?'

He gave a small smile.

'No one will steal my drinks.'

Solid.

She raised a glass, said, 'Cheers.' Downed it and felt the nigh instant hit.

He was staring at her with only a vague disinterest. He said, 'Have another.'

She did.

Then, as she let it jolt, she asked, 'Aren't you having some?'

He flexed his arms – she could see the muscle.

'I'm on another trip.'

Gail was astonished. For the first time in – how long? – she was interested in another person. This guy had some moves.

'Like dope you mean?' she asked.

He moved a glass towards her.

'That's some of it?'

She could see the flames building in the corner of the club, and on impulse asked, 'Do you see . . . flames?'

He said with a knowing look, a half smile, 'I ignite them, that's part of the trip.'

She had to know.

'And the rest of the trip – what's that?'

He leaned over, said, 'I kill people.'

It had been such a long time since she'd felt attracted to a man, indeed to any human being, but this guy, he had a grace, a litheness, like a panther, and that aura of darkness she knew so well.

He drained a tot, stood, said, 'Time for my walk by the ocean.'

Didn't ask if she wanted to come, so she simply followed him.

Outside the club, he hailed a cab and turned to her.

'Aren't you afraid of what I might do?'

The tequila blended nicely with her psychosis and she said, 'You'd need to be good.'

He held the door of the cab for her, said, 'That's what I thought.'

He told the driver to take them to Salthill and sat back, staring straight ahead. She loved that, no need for any of that small-talk shite. She felt a delicious frisson of anticipation as they passed the site of the burned-out car. It was gone now, but she could still summon the vibe.

She said, 'That's where the girl was burned to death.'

He never looked, said, 'Yeah?'

Like he could give a fuck.

He tipped the driver from a wallet laden with cash and it crossed her mind that she might take it later, after she was done with him. As the cab pulled off he said, 'You want money, ask, don't try to take it.'

And then he was heading towards the water.

She giggled, blamed the tequila, said to herself, 'I'm in love.'

They sat and talked for about two hours. He was telling her how the sea washed away everything and then was quiet. She couldn't believe he never made one move on her.

She said, 'In your wallet, I saw a girl. She your wife?'

He shook his head, stood up, said, 'Come on, I'll take you home.'

And took her hand. His touch was electric. She was astounded at herself, letting him do all the running.

He hailed another cab, got the driver to drop her at her address, and as she got out of the cab he said, 'You want to see me again, I'll be at the beach, Friday night, round eleven. I'll bring some booze, some other stuff.'

And she was standing on the footpath, wanting to ask him in.

She asked, 'What's your name?'

He gave her a look of amusement, said, 'Don't get hung up on labels. Seek the essence . . . what lies beneath.'

23

*'All those who consider external things important
are stupid within.'*

Chuang-Tzu

It was early morning. The postman had come, bringing an official-looking letter. I'd made strong coffee, toast but had no appetite, tore open the letter. It was from the estate agent.

I read it in amazement, crunched on a slice of hard toast, tasting nothing. There'd been three offers to buy. The figures were ridiculous. I couldn't actually take in that such amounts of money were available. Galway was reputed to be the most expensive area in the country and the price of houses was beyond insane. All I had to do was say yes to the highest offer and I'd be rich . . . and homeless. The latter was familiar, but the former – how would that feel?

A knock on the door and I put the letter aside, figuring Ridge.

It was Stewart, dressed like civility: smart overcoat, silk scarf loosely tied around the collar, dark stylish pants. His shoes were dazzling in their spit polish.

I asked, 'How did you know where I live?'

His eyes were alight with dark energy.

'Don't be stupid, Jack.'

I moved aside to wave him in. He gave the apartment intensive scrutiny, then spotted the estate agent's heading.

'Selling up?'

I closed the door, said, 'Well, selling out is what I do.'

He sat on the hard chair and I asked if he'd like anything, saying I'd, alas, no herbal tea.

He declined, looked at me, said, 'I found her.'

'Gail?'

'We're dating.'

He had to be fucking joking, though humour was one of the traits he'd left in jail.

I asked, 'You're joking?'

He gave me that odd look, as if he still wasn't quite sure when I was serious.

'In all our odd and colourful history, Jack, you ever knew me to be a kidder?'

A slight edge leaked over his words and I wondered anew what he'd had to shut down, to cut off, to survive in prison. Whatever it was, it wasn't returning.

I shook my head, said, 'Tell me.'

He gave a slight smile. This was the Jack Taylor he was most comfortable with.

'There's the Guard in you still remains. I told you I have contacts, and though I don't deal drugs any more, I know the network and that means knowing where the players hang out. You with me?'

How fucking complicated was it?

I said, 'Gee, I think I can follow it.'

He let that slide.

'So I checked out the clubs, like revisiting my youth, and

third strike, I found her. And I have to tell you, Jack, you didn't do her justice.'

I wasn't sure where he was going with this, but I was sure I didn't like it. I snapped, 'What do you mean?'

He drew a deep sigh.

'My sister, who was killed – and I'll never forget you got justice for her – she was the best person I ever met, true goodness. I think Gail might have once been a little like her, but after her mother died, after the suicide attempt, she died.'

My expression must have shown cynicism.

He continued, 'Sure, she came back, but wherever she was during that time before, someone else came back, a true malevolent being. I met the worst men on the planet in jail – real scum, pure evil, psychos, sociopaths, you name it, every type of dangerous animal – but they are nothing, nothing compared to the sheer power of darkness in this girl.'

I wasn't buying it, said, 'She's just a girl, and a nasty vicious thug. Don't make her out to be some super being.'

Now his smile was full but not warm. He said, 'Good, we're on the same page, my friend. I needed to know you were on board.'

What the hell was this?

I stared at him and he said, 'Jail isn't going to stop her. You have to remove her.'

I was pacing, said, 'Call it what it is: kill her.'

He stood up.

'Here is the address of the house they're renting. On Friday night, she'll be meeting me. Why don't you go and

have a chat with the father and son, and I'll keep the girl
. . . *occupied.*'

I wasn't sure what he was driving at, so I asked, 'And what the hell am I supposed to do?'

He let his shoulders slump, the classic body language of defeat.

'Jack, this is your gig, I'm just along for the ride.'

Fuck.

I said, 'Nothing's exactly that . . . nothing.'

He stopped at the door, taken by surprise.

'Is that Zen you've been studying?'

And that rarity in his tone: delight.

I let him savour it, then said, 'Fuck no, that's Paul Newman in *Cool Hand Luke.*'

24

'Death is Nature's way of telling us to slow down.'

Irish proverb

The address Stewart had given me was in Father Griffin Road, and I figured I better have a look at it. My limp was acting up, so the walk would be good. I walked along Shop Street and buskers, mimes were out in full swing. One mime, raised up on a box, was meant to represent the devil, covered in red paint, with horns, tail and what appeared to be a pitchfork, though it was a little bent – maybe that was the intention. A young boy was staring up at him, transfixed, I stopped for a moment and the devil spoke to me in a Galway accent.

'Want to shake hands with Satan?'

Tempted to tell him I'd been doing that for more years than he'd believe. I put some euros in his box and he gave me a wide grin. His teeth were black, I don't think they were part of the disguise.

I saw a familiar figure coming towards me – Caz, a Romanian who'd been in the city for nearly six years and had become completely acclimatized. He'd learned Irish-English to an amazing degree, he usually tapped me, and somehow got the message across that by taking the money he was doing me a favour. As I said, he'd learned real well.

He greeted me with, 'Jack, me oul' mate.'

Very Romanian, right?

He was dressed in a new suede jacket, designer jeans and very flash cowboy boots. The last time I'd seen him, he'd been expecting deportation. Things had obviously improved, big time.

'Caz, how are you?'

He stared at me, asked, 'What's with the hearing aid?'

What do you say?

I said, 'Old age.'

He nodded, no argument there.

Fuck.

He looked round, as if he'd something important to tell, then 'I'm a little short.'

The touch.

I palmed him some notes, and he quickly put them away.

He said, 'I hear odd stories about you.'

Did I want to know?

I risked it, asked, 'Like what?'

'That you don't drink any more, that you haven't had a drink for donkey's years.'

In Ireland, that is as odd as it gets.

I said, 'Yeah, it's been a while.'

Drinkers hate to lose one of the gang. It's an implied threat that maybe they might be next.

Perish the thought.

He asked, 'How's that going for you?'

Just fucking dandy, a joy a minute.

'It's OK, you get used to it.'

Like fuck.

He scratched his head, pressed, 'What do you do, you know, with all the time?'

I had no idea.

I said, 'I read a lot.'

He began to move away, said, 'You poor bastard.'

Amen.

I did a mini tour of my city. America was looming nearer and I might never again get to walk these streets. I went towards St Joseph's, Presentation Road. I remember my father telling me about the Black and Tans and the British Military lined up outside that church, when Father Griffin had been shot by them in a reprisal. The murder of priests was not part of our history. The difference now was, we no longer needed occupying armies to do it. We were the killers.

The funeral of Father Griffin in 1920 had left Mill Street and crossed O'Brien's Bridge, and there were still old people who swore that as the hearse hit the middle of the bridge, three salmon leaped from the water, hung suspended in mid air for a moment and then slipped gracefully back down. You don't see the salmon leap any more, the poison in the water has them lacklustre, much like the population. My dad, telling me this, his eyes wet, said the driver of the hearse, a guy of rare courage and spirit, wore a top hat and sash in defiance of the ruling edicts. Then and now, I see that man, a hero to his own fierce belief. The following week, he was shot dead.

You ask the young people who Father Griffin was and they give you the look that goes, 'Like, dude, I dunno priests.'

I found the house in Father Griffin Road without any trouble. It's a narrow street and used to be real old Galway. Not any more, but then, what was?

For Sale signs were the main feature now. I had to be real careful. If any of the family spotted me, I was fucked. The house was near the middle, seemed quiet, no movement.

I jumped when a man spoke, asked, 'You looking for someone?'

I turned to face a man in his seventies, with a dog on a leash – I was going to suggest he stay away from Newcastle. He had a bright, alert expression and his accent was local.

I said, 'I was thinking of buying a house.'

He looked at the house, said, 'That one is rented to an English family, but the others, down a bit, they're for sale. You'll need a few bob.'

'What are the English crowd like?'

His face suggested this was a really dumb question.

'They're polite . . . but friendly? They're Brits, they don't know how to do that.'

And he had no more to say on the subject. I thanked him, began to move off.

He added, 'Used to be a real nice street. Didn't everywhere?'

*   *   *

Back home, the man who'd driven Father Griffin's hearse was vivid in my mind and I swear I could see him as I dry-fired the Glock a few times, trying to picture myself using it on Gail. Stewart was right – prison was not the answer for her. But this?

My phone went. Gina, the doctor, inquiring as to how my hands were recovering. I said they were healing well, and then there was silence. I suppose it was the space where I should have asked her if she'd like to maybe get a meal or go out. I wanted to, but couldn't do it. I said I'd give her a call real soon, as soon as I got a few details sorted. Yeah, like kill a young woman. I could tell from her voice she didn't think I was going to call. I thanked her for her concern, sounding like an ungrateful asshole.

I checked my watch. Stewart would be meeting Gail soon and it was time to go call on Mitch and Sean. I put on my Garda all-weather coat, loaded the weapon and put the gun in my right-hand pocket, hoping to hell I wouldn't have to use it on Sean. It's not that I had a liking for that kid, but he was definitely caught up in events he had no control over.

It was dark when I got to Father Griffin Road, lights were blazing all over the house. I debated trying to break in the back way and then thought, the hell with it, I'd take them head on.

I rang the doorbell, my right hand in my coat pocket, gripping the Glock. It was three minutes before the door was pulled open.

Sean stood there, his face ashen, his eyes wide. He gasped, 'My dad, something's wrong with him.'

I thought there was a lot wrong with them all, but went in, asked, 'What do you mean?'

Sean was near hysterical.

'Gail had a huge fight with him. We're running out of money, and she said she'd found a new source. Dad was saying that it might be time to call it quits and she went ballistic, called him a coward and stormed out.'

I was looking to see where Mitch was. I didn't want him coming at me from my blind side.

Sean continued, taking huge gulps of air, 'Dad was clutching at his chest, then he staggered upstairs, and I've been afraid to go up.'

'How long ago was that?'

Sean tried to think, his mind obviously in ribbons. 'Three hours? More?'

I listened: no sound.

I said, 'Wait here, I'll go up.'

'It's the big bedroom, on the right.'

I went up slowly, debating whether I should have the gun drawn, decided to risk not doing so. I went into the bedroom.

It had flock wallpaper, that awful stuff that lined the homes of the poor so long, and on the wall three flying ducks – the middle one was missing its head. The bed was a single and that made me sad, I don't know why, what the fuck difference did it make? But it did. Single beds for adults are symbols of failure. The sheets were dirty and I didn't think they'd be washed now. Laundry, I was fretting about laundry? I thought about what this man, this father was responsible for, the warped children he'd reared, created, and the deeds he'd not only condoned but supervised. I believed he'd orchestrated acts so vile and stomach-churning that it was nigh impossible to imagine what he thought when he lay his head on the pillow at night. Did he think of Nora, his beloved wife? No matter how twisted by grief he'd become, surely he knew that she'd have been horrified at what he'd done in her name, and worse, caused her adored children to carry out.

I whispered, 'You bad bastard, you unleashed the wrath of hell. Did you think you could control it? Well, mate, I hope it's hot enough where you surely are now. And you know what? I hope if there's that afterlife, you never . . . never get to see Nora. Rest in fucking ribbons.'

Sean called up, 'Dad, are you OK?'

I came down, and Sean was staring at me, terror writ on his face.

I said, 'Call an ambulance.'

He didn't move.

'Is he going to be all right?'

'No, he's dead.'

Massive heart attack. He'd been sprawled across the bed, his mouth opened in a silent scream. Sean began to howl. I went to the phone, called 911 then went back to Sean and slapped his face hard.

'Get a grip. I have to go, I can't be here. Just tell them he went to bed and you went to check, found him as he is.'

He nodded, asked, 'What about Gail, what will I tell her?'

I had no idea. I said, 'It will be OK, just wait and do what I told you.'

I got out of there. I could hear a siren. I was halfway down the street when I realized I was still gripping the Glock. I said to myself, 'One down, two to go.'

I passed five pubs, two off-licences on the way home. They sang to me like rarely before.

I kept moving.

25

*'The true religion would have to teach greatness
and wretchedness, inspire self-esteem and
self-contempt, love and hate.'*

Pascal, *Pensées*, 494

I was listening to the morning news a few days after and the death of an English national was reported. It said he'd suffered a coronary but had been dead on arrival at the hospital. The Guards were anxious to get in touch with his son and daughter, who were believed to have been staying with him.

What the fuck?

Sean legged it?

Gail didn't come home?

What the hell?

I tried ringing Stewart, but his mobile was switched off. A terrible thought crossed my mind. What if Stewart had been too smug and Gail took him off the board?

Jesus.

She certainly had the experience. And like a true predator, she could sense danger. I'd made up my mind to go round to Stewart's house when a loud rapping hit my door. I hesitated, then got the Glock, put it in my waistband. Opened the door.

Ridge.

A very agitated Ridge, who launched, 'What is going on?'

And she pushed past me, stood in the middle of my apartment, hands on her hips, accusation writ large.

I closed the door, moved to face her, asked, 'You want to keep your voice down?'

She didn't.

She said, 'Mitchell suffers a fatal heart attack, and then a young woman in her twenties is washed up on the beach, an apparent suicide.'

I had to sit down.

Gail?

The gun dug into my ribs and I took it out, laid it on the table.

She stared at it with disbelief. Took her a few moments, then she went, 'You answer the door armed? Who were you expecting?'

I was trying to get it into perspective.

'Jehovah's Witnesses or Mormons, I'm never sure which is which.'

She looked like she might strike me.

'You think you can joke your way out of this? You're up to your arse here. I know you, it has all the hallmarks of a Taylor fiasco.'

I was suddenly very tired, could already see how it might be read: the father has a massive heart attack and the daughter, grief stricken, drowns herself. Could fly.

I said, 'You told me yourself nothing could be proved against the family, so I backed off.'

She was beyond anger, didn't quite know what to do with me, said, 'You never backed off in your life.'

I wanted her to go so I could think.

I said, 'I think I'm finally beginning to learn.'

She moved to take the gun and I lashed out my hand. 'You don't want to do that.'

A full minute passed as we both held the gun, then she let it go and said, 'Get rid of it. Guns have never been part of your act, and if you get caught with it I won't be able to protect you.'

And I was moved, to hear her say *I won't be able to protect you.*

I was afraid to ask about the tests. If she had the result, would I be able to accept a bad verdict? We stood for a moment, worried about each other for different reasons, and yet a chasm of contorted stubbornness prevented us from reaching, bridging that awful gap. I tried to explain that Gail had come to my apartment a few days earlier and I'd felt I needed protection of my own.

Ridge pondered this.

'But you're not the shooting type. It's not you, Jack.'

Long as our history had been, there were some areas she didn't know about, some acts I'd committed that she'd never understand and that I certainly would never tell her.

I agreed that I'd get rid of it and then I asked, 'Any word on the results?'

Her face near crumpled but she reined it in.

'No, not yet. The waiting gets to you. Every time the post comes, you wonder if there's a letter that will change your whole life.'

I said a thing I never thought I'd ever say to her, said it in an American tone to keep it light.

'I'll protect you.'

And I swear to God, I thought she was going to weep.

But she moved to the door, said, 'I know that, Jack.'

I went to church.

You're Catholic, you're reared to believe that there is sanctuary there. With all the recent scandals, it was less a place of refuge than the belly of the beast. I went to get in from the rain. Had been walking by the cathedral when the heavens opened. Not your soft Irish rain, no, this was a full onslaught of biblical scale, drench-you-to-the-core stuff. The side door was locked, very welcoming, and by the time I got to the main one I was soaked to my skin, muttering, 'Shite and onions.'

That's literary allusion, James Joyce's favourite expression, honest to God.

I dipped me fingers in the holy water font. It was dry, wouldn't you know, and I guess that is some sort of ecumenical irony. I got in, shaking the rain from me sodden clothes, muttering like a lunatic. Told myself it was good to be there, light some candles for Cody, Serena May and the long list of my dead. I hoped they had more candles than holy water.

Time was, I took my candle business to the Augustine till they went techno. Yeah, automated buttons to light your wick. That doesn't do it for me, I need the whole ritual of the taper, the smell of the wax, to see the candle take flame. It comforts me, makes me feel like some items are not for sale.

I lit a whole mess of them, stuffed a wad of notes into the box, watched the candles burn.

Heard, 'A candle is a prayer in action.'

I turned to face a tall priest in his late sixties, with snow-white hair and a face that was not so much lined as seriously creased. He was like a clerical Clint Eastwood.

I asked, 'You believe that?'

I didn't really give a toss what he believed, I was all through with the clergy.

He said, 'It's a lovely thought, don't you agree?'

I was in no mood for being agreeable.

'Seem like just candles to me.'

He considered that, then took me from blindside by asking, 'Would you like some tea?'

'Isn't that what got you boyos in the trouble you're in, issuing invitations like that?'

He took it well, said, 'I don't think I'll be taking advantage of you.'

Good point.

Before I could say that, he added, 'It's only that I don't like to drink my tea alone, and I thought, seeing as you're soaked, you might like to join me.'

I could hear the rain still hammering down so I said, 'Why not?'

He led me to the vestry, and it had a small alcove to the side. He closed the door, began to do tea stuff. He indicated I should sit so I did, on a hard chair, even though there was a soft, well-worn armchair beside it.

He asked, 'You don't want the easier option?'

Priests, you got to watch them, they sneak up on you with loaded questions.

I said, 'I figured that was yours.'

The kettle was boiling, making a sound like friendship, a rare sound to me.

He said, 'But at a guess, you take the hard route most times.'

See, just like I said, sneaky.

He heated the cups – you don't see that any more – then used real tea, Liptons no less, and spread some Hobnob biscuits on a plate, the ones with one side covered in chocolate. I don't know, that alone made me like him. He put the lot on a small table, urged, 'Dig in.'

I asked, 'What do I call you?'

He wiped crumbs from his mouth, put out his hand, said, 'I don't see you calling me Father, so Jim is fine. And you're?'

I took his hand, strong grip.

'Jack Taylor.'

Didn't ring any bells for him, thank God. He poured my tea and I asked, 'How's business?'

He loved that, took a moment to savour it.

'We're having some problems, but I'm optimistic.'

Or an idiot.

I asked, 'Despite all the . . . *problems* . . . what's with the attitude? I mean, the top guys, they're still as arrogant as ever, still issuing pronouncements and what do they call them . . . edicts? What's with that?'

He sighed, admitted, 'Old habits die hard.'

Which was fair enough.

He had a question of his own.

'So what do you do, Jack, beside light a riot of candles?'

A riot, I liked it.

'Mainly, I don't mind my own business, bit like the Church.'

I tried the tea. It was strong, bitter, like the old days, but at least it was familiar. I had another question.

'Where are you on the nature of evil?'

He reconsidered me, gave me a thoughtful scan.

'Odd query.'

'That's an answer?'

He smiled, said, 'I'm playing for time.'

I waited, then he said, 'I believe in it. I've seen it, felt it, and alas, it seems to be on the increase.'

Jesus, he had that right.

I pushed, 'If you knew someone who was truly evil, beyond so-called redemption, what would you suggest?'

He went with the script.

'We believe that no one is beyond saving.'

My turn to smile. 'You're not getting out much, I'd say.'

A bell tinkled and he said, 'The confessional, I'll have to go. Perhaps we might continue this another time.'

I stood up, said, 'What's the penance these days, three Hail Marys and a Glory Be?'

He gave my shoulder a warm grip, said, 'You haven't been for a time, I'd think?'

I said, 'I met the devil in Shop Street the other day.'

He wasn't surprised.

'He does tend to be in the commercial sector. How was he?'

'Bad teeth.'

He enjoyed that. As we headed out, I said, 'He offered to shake my hand.'

'And?'

The rain had stopped. I looked round the church – it seemed warm and I was reluctant to leave, but headed for the door, said, 'Take a wild guess.'

He said, 'Never underestimate the Antichrist.'

I told him I'd bear it in mind.

I continued to ring Stewart's mobile. I was demented with worry. What if Gail had taken him out too? I'd just lost Cody, I couldn't cope with another young guy going down.

It was nearly a week later when he finally answered. 'Yeah?'

I was so stunned to hear him, I didn't speak for a moment and he repeated, 'Yeah?'

'Where the hell have you been?'

'This can only be Jack Taylor. The warmth just seeps from you, Jack.'

I was spitting iron, translate as seriously enraged, shouted, 'What's going on? What happened with . . . you know . . . and where the hell have you been?'

If my anger was affecting him, he was hiding it real well.

'Sorry, hadn't realized I had to report in to you. And where have I been? I've been on retreat.'

I wanted to tell him how worried I'd been, but like Ridge, words stuck in my throat when it came to these moments of vulnerability, and for the thousandth time I asked myself, *What is wrong with you?*

'Retreat? What the fuck does that mean?'

His voice never changed, kept that low pitch. He said, 'Meditating, with a Zen Master, learning to be still. Wouldn't do you any harm, it seems.'

I was so relieved he was alive that I wanted to kill him. Does it get any more Irish than that? I tried to bring down the bile. 'We need to meet.'

He let a silence build.

'Need? That's what has the world so screwed, Jack. We actually don't *need* anything.'

I realized if he kept up this shite, he might well hang up on me, decide to be more still, or stiller?

I took a deep breath. 'May we meet?'

I could hear the amusement in his tone. He said, 'See, you're calmer already. Doesn't that feel better? I'm at home, come round at your leisure.'

The fuckhead.

I said, 'See you in twenty minutes.'

'I'll be here.'

I considered bringing the Glock, putting a bullet in his knee, seeing how still that left him.

A freezing wind was blowing across the city and sleet was promised. I shivered, though I'm not entirely sure it was due to the weather. I was at his place in ten minutes, resolved to keep cool. Rang the bell.

He took his sweet time in answering, then opened the door, said, 'Jack, good to see you.'

Waved me in. He was dressed in some kind of white judo outfit, his feet bare. His home looked even more vacant than before. He asked if I'd like some tea and I said no. He indicated I should sit and he sat on the floor, assumed the lotus position, his features betraying nothing.

Still wanting to kick him in the head, I got straight to it. 'What happened?'

He regarded me with mild curiosity, as if he was seeing me for the first time.

'You mean in the global sense, on the world stage? I can't help you there. My view . . .'

He paused, as if searching for the right word.

'. . . has become more . . . *neutral*.'

He was nuts, just plain crazy. All his previous experiences – his sister's death, jail – had finally got to him and he'd lost it.

I counted to ten, said, 'Gail, the date you had with her, she turned up . . . drowned.'

He nodded, as if he knew but it had slipped from his mind.

He said, 'She had nowhere left to go. The water was cleansing really, took her away from all the torment.'

If he'd said she was now *still*, I'd have battered him senseless.

'Did you help her along?'

He considered this as if it was vaguely interesting, not riveting but maybe deserving an answer.

'Oh Jack, you jump to conclusions, you decide something is the way you want it to be and you make everything else fit into that.'

My patience was real low. I reached into my reserves, tried to find some patch of tolerance.

Nope.

Didn't have it.

And I was up, grabbed him by his judo shirt, hauled him to his feet, then slammed him into the wall.

Hard.

Said, 'Enough with the Zen horseshite. Did you kill her?'

He let his body stay loose, didn't react to my violence, said slowly, 'I was with her on Friday night, remember?'

My fist was clenched, ready to pound him. I wanted to so badly, gritted, 'Yeah. So fucking what?'

His voice was even, measured, the way you talk to an unruly child.

'Jack, she drowned on Sunday night.'

I let him go, moved back, said, 'What?'

He smoothed his outfit, leaned against the wall.

'You really ought to check your facts, Jack. Sunday night, I was on retreat in Limerick with fifty other people.'

I didn't know what to think.

'She committed suicide? Or someone helped her?'

He moved away from the wall, took up his frigging lotus stance again.

'You're the investigator, so . . . investigate.'

I was completely lost.

'I'm totally in the dark.'

He smiled, said, 'For many, that is the true beginning.'

I stormed out before I did serious damage to him.

26

'*Mysterium iniquitatis.*'

'The mystery of evil.'

St Paul

I needed to talk to somebody, to try and get some idea of what was going down.

Gina had experience of psychology, so I gave her a call. She seemed delighted to hear from me. That anyone would be pleased to hear my voice was stunning. I fumbled a bit, finally got round to asking her out to dinner, and arranged to meet her at a new Mexican restaurant she was anxious to try.

What did I know about Mexican food? Then reprimanded me own self. Fuck's sake, this was not about food.

An hour before I met her, I was nervous, my heart hammering. Was this like . . . a date?

How the hell did you behave, and worse, sober? It had been so long, I no longer knew the ritual. And in the days when I did date, I'd slam home a few Jamesons and not give a toss whether the woman showed or not. By the time the evening was through, most of the women were sorry they'd showed.

I wore a blazer, tan slacks, comfortable shoes. For comfortable, read old. I debated a tie and then went with the open-neck gig, casual but cool. Checked my reflection. I looked like a dodgy geezer selling property in Spain.

The restaurant was in Kirwan's Lane, just a pint away from Quay Street. My hands were sweating. Gina was waiting outside, wearing a dark suit jacket, skirt and heels, and looked terrific. Her hair was tied back, showing her strong features. I felt woefully inadequate. She gave me a kiss on the cheek and said I looked marvellous. I wanted to run.

A maître d' told us we'd have to wait ten minutes and might he bring us a cocktail? Bring me a bucket, buddy.

We sat in the lounge. Gina had a Vermouth and soda and yeah, I had a Pepsi. Rock 'n' roll. Gina looked round at the white stucco walls, the cacti, the paintings of old Mexico and said it was very authentic. A couple next to us were lashing back tequila, the whole salt-and-lemon vibe, and having a whale of a time. I felt like a priest and that's about as bad as it gets.

The drinks came and we clinked glasses.

Gina said, 'I'm glad to see you, Jack.'

I wanted to cut to the chase, go, 'Look, I want to pick your brains, can we just do that? Forget all this politeness crap, and then I can go home, alone.'

Very worrying was the fact that I was more attracted to her than I expected. And to handle that without a shot of something, I hadn't a clue. Desperate for time, I asked about her work and she effortlessly talked on that. I tried to show interest. The sound ringing in my ears was the tequila bottle and a rage was building in me. How many fucking drinks were those bastards going to have? Didn't they have dinner to eat yet?

Then I registered Gina asking, 'Is it very difficult for you?'

What?

I gave a smile of tolerance, as if I was resigned to whatever fate had been dealt out to me.

She said, 'A social evening without alcohol, is it awful for you?'

Sympathy, just what I needed, fucking wonderful.

I lied, 'No, it's not so bad.'

The waiter came, said our table was ready and she was prevented from replying.

I let Gina order the food and she chose enchiladas, fritos, tapas, and lots of dips with very spicy origins. She said she'd have a glass of wine, and me, mineral water.

We ate and stayed on neutral topics. I'm sure the food was good. Gina said it was first rate, but it all tasted like loss to me.

When the plates were cleared away and we settled to a coffee, she asked, 'What's on your mind, Jack?'

This was the reason we were there, so I laid out the whole series of events. And she was a good listener, only interrupted once to ask if Sean had turned up yet. I noticed she'd only had one sip out of her wine. Yeah, I counted, it's what alkies do. Me, I'd have been on the third bottle by now.

Go figure.

I can't.

When I was finished, she asked, 'What do you want from me, Jack?'

I framed my reply carefully, said, 'Give me your opinion of the family, and – here's the hard part – where would Sean go?'

She then asked a series of questions, mostly on Gail, and I told her everything – my encounter with her in the graveyard, then her visit to my apartment, the meeting she had with Stewart. I described the father, Mitch, how I'd found him and how I thought he'd been involved.

She was silent for a second round of coffee, then said, 'Jack, it's almost impossible to make any diagnosis when you've never met the people, and anything I say is purely conjecture. I want you to bear that in mind. It's purely guesswork.' Then she smiled. 'To let you in on a little secret, a lot of what we do is a shot in the dark at the best of times, but we don't advertise that.'

I assured her that I wouldn't be quoting her and that any help, any suggestion would be taken in that spirit.

Pushing her cup to one side, she leaned forward and asked, 'Are you familiar with folie à deux?'

I wasn't.

She explained.

'It's a shared psychotic disorder. You get two highly damaged individuals who come to share the same psychotic belief, they become almost one person, with the same destructive aim. There is usually one leader, as it were, and the second person begins to take on board all the delusions, hatred and mania of the first. Fusing together, they form a highly lethal relationship, for example the Hillside Stranglers in America.'

I thought about it, said, 'Gail and her father.'

She nodded, then again stressed this was pure speculation.

I asked about Sean.

She said, 'My bet is he would return to the scene where Gail was drowned, almost like keeping vigil. What are you going to do with him?'

I hadn't been really clear, but now it began to come together.

'If I find him, I'm going to let him go, tell him to get back to London, try and build a life.'

She was surprised, I could see it in her eyes, and she asked, 'Why, don't you think he should pay for his part in these horrendous crimes?'

I was close to telling her of the terrible mistakes I'd made in the past, when I let my madness for revenge override everything and innocent people had died. Instead I said, 'I think there has been enough death.'

The waiter brought the bill and I paid.

Outside I hailed a cab and said, 'Gina, I'm so grateful.'

She was amused. 'I'd hazard another guess and say I'm going home alone.'

I muttered a whole range of nonsense about us getting together real soon and the wondrous help she'd been.

Shite talk.

The cab came and I held the door. She gave me a long look, then said, 'Goodbye, Jack.'

I should have said something, that it wasn't like that, that I'd call her real soon. She gave a sad smile and the cab pulled away.

I walked up Quay Street, telling myself I would call her, course I would. Maybe if I said it often enough, I might actually believe it.

I began the ritual of walking the prom every evening. Gail had been taken out of the water at ten in the evening, so I aimed at that. Part of me saw it as a fool's errand. What if he never showed? Told myself, at least it's exercise, gets me out, gets me moving. And it sure helped with the limp. Her body had been washed up at Blackrock. Time was, that was a men-only bathing area. That had been overturned and women could now use the facilities.

On the beach, most evenings, I'd see groups of teenagers drinking Buckfast, with a token bottle of vodka to put the flourish on the whole deal of getting *wasted*.

My teenage years, it was a flask of cider, split about five ways, and a packet of Woodbine. Dope was unknown then. The new generation, they had lots of dope, from E to coke to crack. Crystal Meth had been showing its ugly dangerous face in more substantial quantities. I'd talked to one of the teenage girls and she told me the deal: none of that slow burn, gradually getting a bit merry, having a rites-of-passage adventure; their whole aim was to get wasted, fast. No in-between time, no period of silly giggles, it was just get totally out of your head in jig time.

I'd asked, 'Why?'

Dumb, right? And old, fuck, oh yeah.

She'd given me that look of contempt with a slight sprinkle of pity and said, 'Cos life, like, sucks.'

She could have fitted right into Miami Beach or any

American frat party. The government was trying to come to terms with the epidemic of teenage pregnancies, sexual diseases, and I thought, one evening alongside the sea front, they could have seen the whole saga unfold.

I thought about Cody a lot: his wild annoying zest for life, his determination to be a private investigator and how my actions had got him killed. The weight of that was sometimes more than I could bear. Such times, despite my limp, I'd walk like a man trying to outrun his thoughts.

A week went by, no Sean, and I was assailed by doubt. Was the whole plan an exercise in futility? I stayed with it. I enjoyed the walk, if nothing else. To be beside the ocean had always soothed me. And Christ, I needed all the help available. Mostly, on those walks, I thought of all the people I'd known and why I was still above the ground.

Ten days into this deal, I met Jeff.

I was so convinced he was gone and I'd never see him again. He'd been my great friend and then I let his daughter fall to her death and he disappeared into the booze, last seen as a homeless person. His wife, Cathy, had been the one who shot Cody. She had known Cody was like my surrogate son. Perhaps that explained why I never went after her for the shooting.

An eye for an eye.

I took her daughter, she took my son.

Fair trade?

The tenth day of my search, I was turning for the walk home when I saw a man sitting on a bench, staring at me, and as I neared, I recognized him.

Jeff.

At first, I thought it was my mind playing tricks. I'd frequently seen someone who looked like him on the streets of the town. This was no mirage, it was him, the long grey hair tied in a ponytail, a long leather coat and his eyes burning into mine. He stood and I didn't know if he'd attack me. Our last encounter, he'd spat in my face.

I stopped about five yards away, a tremor building in my body.

He said, 'I heard you'd been walking this way, same time every evening.'

I didn't ask who told him.

How do you greet a man whose life you've destroyed? *Good to see you* doesn't quite cut it. He looked well, certainly in comparison to how I'd last seen him, a drunk on a park bench, his eyes dead. His eyes now were clear, hard but clear. A fresh scar along the top of his forehead. You live on the street, it's part of the deal. His clothes were clean, and though he'd visibly aged, he seemed in good nick. His hands were deep in his pockets and I concentrated on them.

'Still investigating, Jack?'

I finally found my voice. 'It's all I can do.'

He looked out at the ocean, then said, 'Still wreaking havoc in people's lives then?'

No argument there.

He sighed, said, 'The Guards are looking for Cathy, in connection with that shooting.'

I said I'd heard that and then he asked, 'And you, Jack, are you looking for her?'

His tone was neutral, as if it didn't matter.

'No, I've caused her enough grief.'

He moved a step closer and I had to struggle to stand my ground.

He asked, 'You think that evens the score? That what you think, Jack?'

His use of my name was like a lash. Each time I felt the sting, I said, 'No, I don't think anything can ever . . . *even the score.*'

He was right in my face now, snarled, 'You got that fucking right, pal.'

Then he backed off. I'd have been grateful if he'd walloped me, it would have been easier.

He asked again, as if he needed it in blood, 'Are you going after Cathy?'

'No, I'm not.'

I wanted to know how he'd turned himself round, how he'd come back from the streets, but I couldn't find the words.

He stared at me, as if trying to find out who I was, then he said, 'I loved you, man.'

And he walked away.

The use of that past tense lacerated my soul.

27

Double-cross.

Three nights later, I found Sean. As was my routine now, I'd walked the prom. It was a bit later than my regular time and darkness was falling. I'd reached Blackrock, was about to turn for home when I took a last look at the ocean. Down among the rocks, near the edge of the water, a lone figure. I nearly didn't see him. I took a deep breath and made my way down. He was sitting on a strip of sand and smoking a joint, a tiny cloud of smoke above his head.

Before I could speak, he said, 'Wondered when you'd show up.'

I moved to his right, could smell the strong aroma of the weed. I'd expected him to be like a vagrant, in terrible shape.

Wrong.

He was the picture of health and prosperity, wearing a new heavy coat and new faded jeans. His hair had been cut and his eyes were alight. He offered the spliff.

'Not for me, thanks.'

This amused him and he looked at me. He was playing with the rosary beads that he wore as a bracelet.

He said, 'I went back to the house after my dad was gone and you know what, I found a wad of cash. So I searched some more in Gail's room, found a whole stash of it. They'd been holding out on me, can you believe it?'

I thought about that and then gradually it began to dawn on me, my whole reading of Gail's death was wrong.

'Must have pissed you off.'

He laughed, said, 'Taylor, they'd been pissing me off my whole life.'

His use of my surname was deliberate, letting me know the rules had changed.

Had they ever.

He flipped the end of the spliff into the water. It made a slight fizzle, like the end of the saddest, most worthless prayer, the one you say for your own self.

He said, 'They collected my mum's insurance money, never told me, and me, dumb fuck, thinking we were out of cash. What we were out of was time. At least, they were.'

I asked, 'So you were in the house and Gail came back?'

He stretched, as if this was oh so slightly boring, said, 'Yeah, I told her good old Dad was a goner and she'd killed him. She freaked, and then, the weirdest thing of all the fucking bizarre events in this mad trip, she retreated.'

I wasn't sure what he meant, so echoed, 'Retreated?'

He looked at me, asked, 'You deaf?' Then laughed, said, 'Oh, whoops, the hearing aid. Yeah, she went back to how she was just after Mum died – a vegetable. Went to wherever it was she'd been before, and I figured, this time she wasn't returning. A one-way ticket, you know?'

I could see it. The two dominant figures in his life were gone, and instead of going to pieces, he'd adopted the personalities of both.

'What did you do with her?'

He was quiet for a moment, as if he debated telling me, then said, 'I helped her go swimming.'

And then, the worst sound of all, he giggled. I told myself it was the dope, hoped it was.

He added, 'Thing was, get this, she forgot she couldn't swim. And you know, the crazy bitch, she kept asking me if I saw the flames. I doused them for her.'

I thought of the Glock, sitting snug and useless in the top drawer of my desk.

He said, 'So, Jack, what's your thinking, you going to let this slide? You can walk away, we'll forget we ever had this conversation.'

He was literally measuring me up, and alas, I knew what he saw: a broken-down middle-aged man with a limp and a hearing aid. If I said I couldn't let it go, how hard was it going to be for him to . . . *deal* . . . with me? He was strong, young and had nothing to lose. He'd drowned his own sister, crucified a young man, burned a defenceless girl in her car. Was he going to worry about me?

I said, 'If – and it's a big if – I walk, what are your plans?'

He was surprised, and to my horror I recognized the expression in his eyes. It was like Gail's, and for one eerie moment I wondered if evil could be transmitted thus. He moved real close to me. Was it my imagination or had his shoulders become broader? What had happened to the Kurt Cobain harmless boy I'd met in the coffee shop?

A half smile curled on his lips and he said, 'Hmmm, good question, Jack-o. You know, I think I like it here, but what I wouldn't like is the thought of you shambling round, maybe getting a sudden burst of – what's it you Catholics call it? – conscience.'

And he lashed out with his right fist, knocking me on my back. He walked round so he was standing at my head. I noticed he was wearing Doc Marten's, well-scuffed ones, and I hoped to fuck they weren't the steel-toed variety. My jaw hurt like a son of a bitch and I understood he was going to kill me but was in no great hurry. He had discovered the greatest, most potent aphrodisiac on the planet – power. I moved to try for some distance and he kicked me on the back of my head.

Hard.

I saw stars. Not the spangled variety, but the ones that tell you you are in deep shit and it's not going to get any better.

He asked, as if he actually cared, 'Did that hurt, Jack?'

Then two more swift kicks to my side and chest, and I felt something give – a rib, perhaps. My breathing tightened.

He said, still in that pleasant conversational tone, 'I've often wondered what it's like to kick the living daylights out of a person. All my life, I've been the one getting kicked, and you know what? You know what, Jack-o? It's kinda neat, as the Americans might say.'

And that galvanized me. America . . . my new life,

Ridge's tests, not being there for her, all because of this – pup?

I groaned, 'Sean, one thing.'

He hesitated, and I kept my voice low so he had to bend over. He still couldn't hear me and bent real low. His face was in mine, I could smell garlic off his breath. I clamped my teeth on his nose, bit down with all the ferocity I've ever known, and swear to Christ, I bit clean through.

He staggered back, blood pumping down his face, going, 'What the fuck did you do? You bit me!'

I managed to get up on one knee, saw a clump of driftwood, hoped the water hadn't softened it.

It hadn't.

And I blasted it across his skull, saying, 'Don't call me Jack-o.'

A few more wallops of pure, unadulterated rage and his face and head were mush.

I muttered, 'We don't want you in our town, we have enough garbage as it is. How do you think we're going to win the tidy-towns competition?'

Had I gone insane? I can only hope so.

I gathered some stones, a lot of very heavy ones, piled them into the pockets of his new smart coat and dragged him to the water. Then, to my horror, he groaned, and I don't know for sure but it sounded like, 'Please, Dad, don't.'

It took a while but eventually he was struggling no more. I took him way out, as far as I could manage without going under my own self. It was cold. With the amount of rocks in his pockets, it was hard work and I nearly abandoned it, but I had to be sure he wouldn't surface. When I was sure he would stay down, I took a deep breath and went under with him, his eyes staring at me like a mild reproach, and added more stones from the bottom of the sea bed. My teeth were doing a fandango of fear and shock. I felt that seeping numbness that whispers to you, 'Rest, let the water soothe you.'

The temptation was massive, but with a supreme effort I put the last of the rocks on him and broke the surface, gasping for air. I looked at how far I'd come and wasn't even sure I'd make it back to shore, then muttered, 'Just do it, stop whining.'

I came out of the water and the inclination to lie down was overpowering, but I managed to keep going. The pain in my head, chest and side was beyond belief. I swallowed a whole shitpile of Stewart's pills, kept moving.

I was nearly home when I realized something from Sean had snagged on my jacket: the rosary beads he'd worn as a bracelet. It had that tiny cross on it.

I was passing a litter bin, put it in there.

I was all through with crosses.

28

Almost a clean getaway.

The following Monday, a man in his twenties came to inspect the flat and finalize the deal. He did a thorough walk around, even pounded the walls. He was representing a businessman named Flanagan.

He said, 'Mr Taylor, I don't see any problems. We'll get our engineer to examine it, of course, but I think we're set. I'm prepared to write you a cheque now for the deposit.'

Here it was, the actual moment, and I baulked. Did I really want to do this? My tickets for America had arrived a few days before and I'd shoved them in a drawer. The money to be paid for the apartment stunned me, but it also meant I'd be homeless.

I asked the guy, 'What will Mr Flanagan do with this?'

He seemed to find that an odd question.

'What do you care?'

I cared.

Mrs Bailey, my one-time landlady, constant friend and supporter, had left it to me.

I gave the guy a look and he said, 'Well, he has a son

coming up to college age, so maybe he'll keep it for him, or perhaps just as a little place in town for overnight stays. You can't go wrong with property in the centre of town.'

That bothered me a lot.

He sensed my unease.

'You do want to sell, Mr Taylor?'

I said, 'Yeah, sure.'

And got rid of him.

I was imbued with a sadness, a melancholy as heavy as the stones I'd laden Sean with.

My passport was renewed and the photo in it made me look like a furtive ghost. I'd nothing to get rid of. Gail had burned my books and I'd long ago burned most of my boats. My goodbyes . . . yeah, they'd take all of two minutes. I was restless, got out of the flat, walked down the town, asking myself, 'Will you miss it?'

I didn't know.

I went into a coffee shop. Knew if I went into a pub, I'd definitely drink and that would solve all my travel problems. I ordered a latte and blocked all thoughts of recent events from my mind. As my coffee arrived, so did Stewart. He asked if he could join me, and I got the waitress to bring him a herbal tea. He was wearing a business suit, expensive shirt and tie. When you've bought cheap all your life, you know what's quality. He seemed completely at ease.

He said, 'So, Jack, you find Sean?'

A small smile was playing around his lips.

I said, 'No, no luck there.'

He thanked the waitress for his tea, then said, 'Must have gone back to London, you think?'

'I've no idea.'

To get him off this track, I told him about the sale of the flat and my emigration plans. He asked who was buying my place.

When I told him, he frowned.

'What?' I asked.

'I'm just a little surprised at you, Jack, you being an advocate of old Galway, the keeper of the Celtic flame, all that good stuff. This guy, this Flanagan, he's a speculator. He'll turn your place into bedsits, shove three non-national families in there.'

I felt raw, he'd touched a nerve. I knew it was not what Mrs Bailey would have wanted. She hated greed and ruthlessness, and here I was, part of the new deal.

I tried, 'Three bedsits? You couldn't swing a cat in my home.'

He smiled. 'I doubt pets will be allowed.'

Then he said, 'I've been keeping an eye on you. I notice you've stopped your nightly walk.'

I felt my heart accelerate.

'Following me? Why?'

'I owe you, Jack, have to ensure you're safe.'

I kept my voice low, said, 'Don't follow me, OK?'

I stood, put a few notes on the table.

He asked, 'Was the water cold?'

I froze. A moment of that utter stillness again, then Ridge passed through my mind and, yeah, my heart.

I walked out.

Muttered, *Don't think, just walk.*

There was a busker outside The Body Shop, doing a real fine version of 'Crazy'. I waited till he finished, took what coins I had and put them in the cap he'd before him.

He looked at it, counted it, went, 'The fuck is that?'

I said, 'It's all I've got.'

He was angry. 'You get a live version of my act and that's what you think it's worth?'

I had to rein myself in. Arguing with a busker, it was a no-win situation. I said, 'Have a good one.'

He shouted, 'Yeah, with that fortune, maybe I'll buy a new car.'

It wasn't helped by the fact he had a Brit accent.

It answered my earlier query about missing Galway.

The next few days, I put the finishing touches to my travel arrangements. I had to see my solicitor, sign the deeds of sale, I'd arranged for the money to be transferred to America when it came through. I packed one suitcase. Looking at it, sitting in the hall, ready to roll, it seemed forlorn, the remnants of a life of waste.

I went to the cemetery to say goodbye to my dead. It was too late to say sorry. The rain had stopped and a furtive sun was teasing the sky. I walked among the headstones, and after I'd said my pathetic words to the ones I loved, I decided to visit the graves of Maria and her brother, asking myself, 'Did I get justice for them?'

A young man was standing near the freshly turned clay and his resemblance to Maria was uncanny.

I approached, said, 'Rory?'

He wasn't startled. I suppose after what had happened to his family, he was beyond shock. He looked at me, his eyes wet, tears on his cheeks. He sighed, asked, 'Are you the Guards?'

More's the Irish pity, not any more.

I said, 'I was a friend of your sister's.'

He was only a young man, but his whole body had the suggestion of age that has nothing to do with time and everything to do with horror.

I asked, 'What took you so long?'

He had no answer, went with, 'Did Maria tell you the full story?'

I wasn't sure how to answer so said, 'I'd like to hear it from you.'

He nodded, as if that was fair. 'The car that killed Mrs Mitchell?'

He was talking about the hit and run that set all of this in motion.

I said, 'Be a man. After all that's happened, at least take responsibility.'

He lowered his head. 'I did. My girlfriend was driving and she had two strikes against her, so I told them I was driving. And then I ran.'

Jesus Christ.

I debated telling him that his lie had cost the lives of all his family and others. Then I thought, fuck it, and began to walk away.

He shouted, 'Are you going to tell on me?'

I didn't answer.

*   *   *

The morning of my departure, I was about to disconnect the phone when it rang. I had a short time to kill before my cab was due to take me to the airport, so I picked it up.

'Jack?'

Ridge.

I hadn't said goodbye to her.

I said, 'Yeah?'

She took a deep breath. I could tell she'd been crying. 'Jack, I need your help.'

I was thinking of *Terms of Endearment*. Jack Nicholson at the airport, smiling in that way only he can and saying he's almost made a clean getaway.

I sat on my suitcase, my heart pounding, and for the first time ever I used an endearment with her.

'What's up, hon?'

'The biopsy, it's malignant.'

Must have been the sunlight coming through the window. I wiped at my eyes, my cheeks wet.